DESERT HONKYTONK

DESERT HONKYTONK

THE STORY OF TOMBSTONE'S BIRD CAGE THEATRE

Roger A. Bruns

FULCRUM PUBLISHING
Golden, Colorado

Library of Congress Cataloging-in-Publication Data

Bruns, Roger.
Desert honkytonk : the story of Tombstone's Bird Cage Theatre / Roger Bruns.
   p. cm.
Includes bibliographical references and index.
   ISBN 1-55591-416-0
   1. Bird Cage Theatre (Tombstone, Ariz.)—History. 2. Performing arts—Arizona—Tombstone—History—19th century. 3. Tombstone (Ariz.)—History—19th century. 4. Tombstone (Ariz.)—Social life and customs. I. Title
   PN2277.T572 B573 2000
   792'.09791'53—dc21   00-009660

Printed in the United States of America
0 9 8 7 6 5 4 3 2 1

Editorial: Daniel Forrest-Bank, Don Graydon
Design: Rudy Ramos
Cover images: Nola Forest at the Bird Cage Theater; inset—prospector in front of the Bird Cage Theater. (Both photographs courtesy of the Arizona State Historical Society, AHS #28244 and AHS #29946.)

Fulcrum Publishing
16100 Table Mountain Parkway, Suite 300
Golden, Colorado 80403
(800) 992-2908 • (303) 277-1623
www.fulcrum-books.com

Contents

Prologue

Within her gilded cage confined,
I saw a dazzling Belle,
A Parrot of that famous kind
Whose name is NON-PAREIL.
                    —WILLIAM WORDSWORTH, 1825

I t was the wickedest night spot, many said, between Basin Street and San Francisco's Barbary Coast. Through the doors of Tombstone's Bird Cage Theatre walked hard-rock miners, cowboys, railroad men, outlaws and lawmen, immigrants, soldiers, speculators, entrepreneurs, and assorted drifters, all looking for amusement in the developing West.

The story of the Bird Cage is the story of people from many elements of the frontier, from the silver mines to the ranches, from the opium parlors to the gambling dens. This book will look at those who gathered late at night in the smoky, riotous confines of the famous night spot, their beer and whiskey flowing, listening to the singers, dancers, magicians, and comedians, hooking up with the sporting ladies who helped make the grind of the hard days fade away.

This story of the Southwest's most notorious variety house, home of Western vaudeville and burlesque, offers a glimpse into the characters who marched through its swinging doors in the days of gaslights and six-guns. Situated in dangerous Apache country, Tombstone with its lure of silver riches became in the space of a few years a central boomtown of the Southwest. From the perspective of the Bird Cage and the lives of the assorted individuals who gathered there, we can see the social dynamics more clearly, the challenges, hopes, and fears of the many different people who made their lives on the frontier.

Tombstone became legendary in later years, mostly because of one thirty-second gunfight down the street from where the Bird Cage Theatre was under construction—an incident kneaded and embellished by later writers and moviemakers and exploited by unbridled commercial hoopla. The Bird Cage itself also became legendary because of flimflam. Despite the claims of local advertising still to be heard in the tourist traps of Allen Street, neither Jenny Lind nor Lillian Russell ever appeared at the Bird Cage. But the place never needed hype and exaggeration. It had its own history and that is quite enough.

CHAPTER 1

A Naughty Establishment

You could hear the raucous music and the shouts and laughter a long way down Allen Street. The eager crowd of men trying to enter or exit gave the doors of the box-shaped, adobe establishment at the end of the street no rest. Inside, the sound ratcheted higher—the piano and violins, the clanking of beer mugs and glasses, the clattering of poker chips and dice, cards fanning, laughter, the loud conversations, all of them vying to be heard. The smells were distinct, sometimes overpowering. Clouds of cigar smoke mixed with the odors of beer and whiskey, overpowering perfume, cheap cologne and, in the case of most of the men, the lack of it.

It is not surprising that the customers who filed into the confines of the Bird Cage were almost entirely men; indeed, the population of Tombstone, as with any new boomtown, was almost entirely male. Without cultural pretension, the Bird Cage Theatre knew its clientele and had its own mission—to cater to the purposes of those who, night after night, burrowed themselves in its dark confines, wrapped up in the loudness and excitement in the quest for pleasure. Here, amidst the din and depravity, they looked for whatever sparks that life in this isolated desert could offer.

The Bird Cage Theatre in Its Heyday. (From a painting by Ross Stefan; courtesy of the Arizona State Historical Society.)

From its earliest days, the place gave off an unbounded aura of naughtiness, a sensual siren's call that drew a steady stream of eager men, some of whom looked uneasily both ways before entering. It was the sauciest jewel of the many hot spots of Allen Street. Rosa Schuster, who lived near the Bird Cage as a young girl, later remembered the men briskly walking up Allen Street and lining up to enter the racy playhouse.

"Almost every man wore mustaches like Texas cow horns, and beards were in style," she said. "The tinhorn gamblers usually trimmed theirs and slickened 'em down with grease or wax, while the common let them wander where they would. Anyway, they all looked more masculine and impressive than the smooth-faced rascals of today."

As the amusement- and lust-starved men of Tombstone entered the lobby of the Bird Cage, they immediately faced a sign: "NOTICE! All

Persons Entering This House are Requested to Divest Themselves of All Weapons in Accordance With Act 13, Section 7, of the Revised Statutes of Arizona." The men obediently unloaded their arsenal of large weapons; the smaller ones stayed hidden: the brass knuckles, daggers, bowie knives, and derringers. Especially ingenious was the "protector," a small gun that could be concealed in a hand, with only the barrel protruding between the fingers.

In the hot, close air, in the dim light of flickering gas jets, red-coated bartenders poured nothing but Tombstone's best at the highly polished, custom-made cherrywood bar. Charley Keene, head bartender as well as stage manager and comedian, presided over his domain like a cleric tending a shrine. At one end of the gleaming surface was a dumbwaiter contrivance that conveyed drinks to the boxes above. Through the evenings, the stock of wines and liquors was continually replenished from the storeroom below the stage. Like many establishments in Tombstone, the choice of whiskeys was plentiful.

Behind the bar was a luxurious painting of a well-rounded, buxom belly-dancer named Fatima, an exotic who once graced the Bird Cage dance boards. So mesmerized was the clientele that she was commemorated by this giant oil. Thousands of men over the years sidled up to that bar, called for a drink, and toasted the swirling Fatima, symbol of the Bird Cage's devilish delights. The painting would later carry the scars of six bullet holes, and a knife slash that added an extra fold in Fatima's skirt.

In saloons and honkytonks across America, the bleary eyes of patrons rested gratefully on similar barroom nudes. Many of these works were the only pieces of original art that western miners and cowboys ever saw. And Fatima had class, certainly more class than one well-known creation in a Denver saloon. In this artistic triumph, the painting of the classic nude was reinforced with rubber hoses. With the slightest squeeze, the painting sprayed unsuspecting customers.

Echoes of the Barbary Coast

After an engagement at the Bird Cage, Comedian Eddie Foy, who had played much larger auditoriums and variety houses around the country, said the place, at least in appearance, resembled a coffin.

Actually, the Bird Cage resembled a number of variety halls in San Francisco's Barbary Coast section, the notorious red-light district by the bay, where prostitutes, gambling, drink, drugs, and other sinful pleasures beckoned to sailors fresh off the hundreds of ships docked at the city, as well as to card sharps, rounders, farmhands, and others seeking shady entertainment. Here in the Barbary Coast, morality took a holiday. It was, the San Francisco *Call* reported, "the last resort of the blasé and ruined *nymphe du pavé*, the home of vice. . . ." Writer Ambrose Bierce declared it to be "a moral penal colony. It is the worst of all the Sodom and Gomorrahs in our modern world."

Such establishments as the Bella Union and Tivoli's offered San Franciscans a riotous blend of leg shows, music, gambling tables and, on mezzanines, private, curtained boxes where patrons could mingle with the dancers and female waiters. The Bella Union advertised its wares in San Francisco newspapers with much gusto. Come to the Bella Union and find "Plain Talk and Beautiful Girls! Really Girly Girls! No Back Numbers, but as Sweet and Charming Creatures As Ever Escaped a Female Seminary. Lovely Tresses! Lovely Lips! Bosom Forms! at the BELLA UNION . . . And Such Fun! If You Don't Want to Risk Both Optics, Shut One Eye!"

Describing a visit to the Bella Union, a reporter recalled walking through a large barroom into a theater surrounded by a circle of curtained boxes that resembled "so many pigeon holes," which could be purchased for fifty dollars a night. He talked about licentious, even profane, songs and dances performed on the stage. He talked about sitting in one of the boxes when one performer, a "pretty little danseuse" he had just seen on stage, suddenly appeared, to hawk, with much sensuous coaxing, the most expensive spirituous liquor dispensed by the house. The word around the West Coast was that the Bella Union, with its high-kicking, nearly undressed ballet girls, worshiped the calf—the female leg variety, not the bovine. "Fullgrown People Are Invited to Visit the Bella Union if You Want to Make a Night of It. The Show is Not of the Kindergarten Class but Just Your Size, if You Are Inclined to Be Frisky and Sporty."

Not only did the interior of the Bird Cage Theatre resemble the Bella Union and other halls in the San Francisco tenderloin, but several of the entertainers who played the Bird Cage had also played the Barbary Coast. Bird Cage proprietor Billy Hutchinson had seen the enormous crowds that flocked to these variety theaters of San Francisco. When he created his own haven amidst the creosote bushes of the Arizona desert, he incorporated the look and feel of San Francisco buildings and he brought along some of the entertainers.

When the Bird Cage first opened, the *Tombstone Epitaph* reported that "Billy Hutchinson will guarantee satisfaction to the lovers of amusement . . . his troupe are unrivaled on the Pacific coast." If the latter part of the statement was hyperbole, the first part was not. The Bird Cage did satisfy the lovers of amusement, those with an itch to be "Frisky and Sporty." It satisfied them the same way that the variety halls satisfied hordes of men in San Francisco. The Bird Cage was a Barbary Coast variety hall planted in the Arizona desert.

The men came to the Bird Cage for the liquor, gambling, music, humor, and entertainment, but mostly they came for the women. Some early variety halls began to display "living statuary," in which women posed in revealing tights as classical subjects. After a night at the Bird Cage, a reporter for the Tombstone *Daily Nugget* described the dancers, hostesses, and actresses of the Bird Cage as "living pictures; which are models of live grace and beauty."

Regular customers of the honkytonk awaited the arrival of the newest Bird Cage entertainers with intense anticipation. Groups of miners, tradesmen, cowpunchers, tinhorn gamblers, and other patrons of the Bird Cage often gathered to cheer and leer as the incoming stagecoaches brought the latest doves from San Francisco.

And the entertainment more than satisfied those with a taste for the risqué. After an early performance at the Bird Cage, one reporter seemed breathless. From belly-dancing odalisques in revealing, striped Turkish pantaloons to winsome, coy lines of girls in bloomers and elaborate garters, the place rocked. "Shortly after midnight," the reporter said, "the curtain rang up on the cancan in all its glory. As the cancan girls retired three men clad in tights with women's undergarments over them sprang to the stage and vied with each other in the obscenity of their actions. . . ."

Bucking the Tiger

In the gambling area of the honkytonk, all manner of players elbowed their way to the tables, jostling for action—the silk-shirted high rollers, the rough miners fresh from the diggings, the cardsharps posing as green amateurs. They played high-stakes poker in the Bird Cage all night long. But most popular were the faro tables, where men played a game that had been popular in France as early as the mid-seventeenth century, at a time when the backs of French playing cards often bore the likeness of an Egyptian ruler. The game was often spelled *pharaoh* or *pharo*. Other early faro cards displayed a portrait of a Bengal tiger and led to such expressions as "bucking the tiger" or "twisting the tiger's tail." In later years, a picture of a tiger often hung outside those gaming houses that offered faro inside.

Hunkered over the tables, they bucked the tiger with cigars hanging loosely from their lips, drinks close by, eyes riveted on the next play, lost in concentration. Here, in this part of the Bird Cage, the sounds were muffled and muted, the energies submerged in raw tension. The next play could be the one that could make them or break them. Even when scantily clad performers brushed against the players, many of them didn't notice. The various pleasures at the Bird Cage were often compartmentalized by the men, as if individual stimulants acted upon different parts of the brain. The card room was for cards; the faro tables were for faro; other parts of the place were for other kinds of frolic.

Vice for Sale

Overhanging two sides of the theater itself, the balcony, divided into fourteen boxes or cribs, glowed with heavy, red velvet drapes and glittering trimmings and jutted from the wall. The boxes afforded an excellent view of the stage. Access to the boxes was gained by narrow stairways leading from the area of the bar. It was in these small rooms, these cribs suspended above the theater, that the Bird Cage ladies of the night plied one particular aspect of their trade. On August 18, 1882, Tucson's *Arizona Star* explained that the way the Bird Cage got its name was simple: the boxes had many doves in them.

Only in physical height were the rooms elevated; they were certainly not elevated in erotic atmosphere. Each of the tiny cribs had a bed and table with a gas lamp, and was decorated in typical shabby boudoir red and black, the bare rudiments of sensuality. Up and down the stairs to the suspended boxes, men climbed with their escorts for a brief interlude—for that time when to be a drifter, a miner, a teamster, or a day laborer in this small town in the remote Southwest was not a time without a woman.

Using all the feminine charms in their arsenal, the girls encouraged the men to purchase expensive liquors. For each round of drinks, a girl earned tokens that could be redeemed at the end of the evening for cash. The women sipped tea colored to look like whiskey as they encouraged their clients to imbibe greater and greater quantities, and pretended to match them glass for glass. The more liquor the customers consumed, the more tokens the ladies earned.

For the women, the encounters in the boxes were business transactions to be endured, to be emotionally blocked out, to be manipulated for greater profit. For most of the men who frequented the Bird Cage, the encounters were also strictly business. The women, of course, had their own stories, many of heartbreak and genuine pathos. But in the Bird Cage they dressed up as fantasies come alive, illusions made real in cheap rouge and red feathers.

For quick assignations, many of the girls led clients to an area behind drapes off a stairway backstage leading to the balcony. Downstairs, below stage level, the Bird Cage had bordello spots more inviting for big spenders. When some of the gamblers hit big at the tables, they didn't head for the lofted cribs or arrange for quick action behind the drapes; they headed for some spacious rooms in the establishment that offered luxuries available only at the more expensive houses of pleasure in Tombstone. With full-size beds, mirrors artfully located, and erotic paintings, these quarters came at a high price, both for the room and for the services of the ladies.

Prior to keeping those dates behind the drapes, in the cribs, and in the bordello rooms, the women danced, sang, or played some supporting role in the house entertainment. During the days, they became adept at designing and sewing their own costumes and even helped construct stage sets and other paraphernalia used in the productions.

Workers from the Lucky Cuss and other mines, storekeepers, cow-punchers, and soldiers mixed with stage drivers, laborers, doctors, and lawyers to get as close as possible to the action they most preferred. The room was a sea of hats in a choking fog of cigar smoke, the clinking of brandy and whiskey glasses barely audible in a din of sound that rose and fell with the actions on stage.

Set about six feet above the lower floor, the stage was big enough to accommodate dancers, magicians, and other theater performers. Bathed in the light of gas jets along its front—with a proscenium opening of about fifteen feet, a height of more than ten feet, and a depth of about fifteen feet—the stage, although cramped, was the scene of a wild variety of acts, from dervish-like fast dancers to athletic acrobats. It had enough room for teams of healthy young women in tights and abbreviated costumes to turn the cancan into a roaring and yet very suggestive workout.

It even had enough area for Lizette, The Flying Nymph, to swing majestically from the Bird Cage heights, over the heads of gaping and gasping patrons, on a suspended cord from one side of the auditorium to the other. Lizette had come to Tombstone as part of the Monarch Carnival Company. Just a few years earlier another carnival performer, Ella Richter, known as Mlle. Zazel, had been shot sixty feet out of a cannon and became known as The Human Cannon Ball. Although springs and not gunpowder had actually blasted Mlle. Zazel into the air, most audiences did not care. The number of human cannonballs in the United States increased dramatically.

The sight of the lithe and luscious Lizette flying overhead proved almost as dramatic to the men in the Bird Cage audience as any cannonball performer. The kind of trapeze stunts she performed at the Bird Cage became so popular in variety shows across the country that Thomas Edison, in his early years of producing motion pictures, set one of his scenes on the stage of a theater. One of Edison's film catalogs described the action:

A lady dressed in evening costume is performing on a trapeze. Two Rubes are seated in a box in the theatre. The lady begins to disrobe and here the fun commences. As she removes her garments one by one and throws them at our rural friends, they begin going through antics, which to say the least, are highly amusing. When the stockings come off, the climax takes place. The Rubes jump from their seats and make things lively for a short time in the theatre.

Historian Walter Noble Burns, in *Tombstone: An Iliad of the Southwest,* a book noteworthy for legend-making, did set an accurate scene for the Bird Cage stage: "Seated on wooden benches, the audience guzzled whiskey and beer and peered through a fog of tobacco smoke at vaudeville performers cutting their capers in the glare of kerosene-lamp footlights. Beautiful painted ladies in scanty costumes sang touching ballads of home and mother on the stage and then hurried to the boxes. . . ."

Will Curlew dressed for a masquerade ball. (Courtesy of the Tombstone Courthouse State Historic Park.)

Nestled up against the stage, several musicians with no Carnegie Hall experience but with a wide repertoire and much energy set the pace for the din that pervaded the establishment. During the rollicking numbers such as "When Johnny Comes Marching Home," the orchestra blasted away, mixing with the clapping, foot stomping, and whistling of the crowd, and the decibels soared. During the weepy, sentimental numbers such as "In the Evening by the Moonlight," the heartrending songs about drifting and lost love, a relative hush settled in, tears welling in the eyes of some of the more liquored patrons.

For the whiskey- and beer-guzzling crowds packed into the theater, the sights on stage, especially the scantily clad chorus girls, were enough to overturn already tipsy equilibriums. Here were red-feathered, flashy-gartered, low-bodiced dancers in fishnet stockings and scarlet satin shoes, winking with suggestive exaggeration, and shaking the boards with rousing cancan numbers, aided by the blasts of the small but spirited orchestra. Here were female acrobats in revealing costumes backflipping from one side of the stage to the other only a few feet from wide-eyed guys who had spent hot, tortuous days deep in the mines. The Bird Cage was their reward.

Also here were lowbrow comedians matching the demands of their low-brow clientele. Here the delirious partygoers could belt out a ribald version of a Son of a Gamboleer" with the gusto it so richly deserved.

Successful performers were often rewarded with a generous showering of coins or folding money on the stage. Other entertainers were not so accomplished or rewarded; they felt the sting of jeers and catcalls. A night at the Bird Cage could be traumatic. A newspaper editorialist later wrote that a middling or embarrassing stage artist "took the chance of having his folks notified of their loss."

In the Gilded Cages

She's only a bird in a gilded cage,
A beautiful sight to see.
You may think she's happy and free from care,
She's not, though she seems to be.

Poignant, a Victorian tearjerker if ever there was one, "She's Only a Bird in a Gilded Cage," officially composed in 1900 by Harry Von Tilzer, with words by Arthur J. Lamb, became one of the nation's most popular songs at the turn of the century.

But there is another story. Shortly after the opening of the Bird Cage, so this story goes, the lyricist Arthur Lamb stood at the bar with the great variety-show entertainer Eddie Foy, who had begun a series of appearances on the Bird Cage stage. Foy made his remark to Lamb that the place seemed like a coffin, long and narrow. Lamb said that the women in their scanty clothes and feathers reminded him of birds in gilded cages.

Struck by the image, Foy remarked, "Sounds like a title to a good song." Inspired, Lamb began to write the words on a napkin from the bar. Later that afternoon, the composer sat at a Bird Cage piano, putting his new song to music. Sidling up to Lamb, Foy praised the effort and said that it would be best sung by a woman. A short time later, Lamb, according to the story, gave the song to a beautiful, heretofore unknown singer, who introduced it on the stage of the Bird Cage. The crowd, it is said, roared its approval, encouraging the singer to make eight encores. The song was "She's Only a Bird in a Gilded Cage" and the singer was Lillian Russell. According to the story, the Bird Cage had launched one of the most recognized songs of the late nineteenth century—and also the career of one of the nation's foremost variety stage performers.

Other versions of the story also claim that when the Bird Cage first opened, it was under the name of the Elite Theatre and that the creation of the song itself led to the change of the establishment's name to the Bird Cage.

There are numerous problems with the story. First, despite the enduring legend, we have an absence of enduring evidence. The lyrics themselves bear almost no relationship to the image of the Bird Cage doves in the curtained boxes. And there is no evidence that Lillian Russell ever appeared at the Bird Cage; most certainly her career was not launched in Tombstone after the opening of the Bird Cage but was launched in New York where she had played on Broadway, both as a theatrical performer and in burlesque as an "English ballad singer."

There is also strong evidence that it was not until 1900 that Von Tilzer put Lamb's words to music. In fact, when Lamb first showed the lyrics to Tilzer, the composer said that he would not write the music unless the story was changed so that the girl in the song was not the rich man's wife, but his mistress. Finally, a check of the Tombstone newspapers of the period clearly reveals that the name of the theater from its beginning in December 1881 was the Bird Cage. When it came under new management several years later, its name was changed briefly to the Elite Theatre. But Billy Hutchinson did not need Arthur Lamb to give him inspiration for the name of his honkytonk.

Like other myths swirling in the historical netherworld of Tombstone of the 1880s, it persists. The irony, of course, is that the Bird Cage never needed legends at all.

Something for All

A Special Correspondent for the Tucson *Star* wrote about his first night in the place:

> After depositing two bits with the door-keeper, I entered a hall
> filled with old age, middle age, bald-head age (next to stage),
> youthful age, and boy age—all sitting around tables drinking
> promiscuously with the "cats." I seated myself at one of them and

was surveying the gallery when a dizzy dame came along and seated herself alongside of me and playfully threw her arms around my neck and coaxingly desired me to set 'em up. All knowing my bashful and guileless ways can imagine my "set back." I thought that all the congregated audience had their eyes on me, and the hot blood surged through my cheeks. Her bosom was so painfully close to my cheeks that I believed I had again returned to my infantile period. To escape from this predicament I immediately ordered them up. She and I, after drinking the liquid, parted at last—she in search of some other gullible "gummie."

For some the place became more than an oasis; it became an obsession. George Parsons, writing about a friend who kept returning night after night, said, "At Bird Cage all of the time—champagne and women. I saw enough tonight to satisfy me about the way R's funds have gone. Too bad, too bad."

A writer for the *Missouri Republican* wrote of his own visit: "The Bird Cage was the soul of Tombstone at night. If you wanted to meet a leading lawyer, a mine or mill superintendent, the sheriff of the county, the chief of police, the mayor of the city, the editor of any of the daily papers, or any of the bright stars of desperadodom, the chances are that if you penetrated the Bird Cage you would have found them."

Indeed, a reporter for the *Star* claimed that Billy Hutchinson's "masquerade balls" attracted all sorts of Tombstone's population that otherwise would have avoided the place for fear of detection:

Monday night last a *bal masque* was given at the Bird Cage under the auspices of its manager, Billy Hutchinson. It was an advent in town that couldn't be missed, as it gave an opportunity to deacons and other religious people to get a peep into the inner workings of the Cage, which I am assured was taken advantage of by a large number, as several in the crowd were pointed out and their names given me, but for the sake of the town's morals I will not expose them, as it would kick up a mess in society circles and add fuel to the collected stock of scandal-mongers.

Making it clear that he saw no reason why a deacon should not have the same rights to enjoy the Bird Cage as any other resident of Tombstone, the reporter concluded: "As the ball advanced and diversion grew interesting, staid old citizens, who never before were seen to frequent like places became hilarious, under the combined pressure of madams and so much feminine loveliness exposed to them. . . . Like amusements were indulged in til old Sol rose in all his majestic glory in the early morn when the godly as ungodly took themselves away to dream of Bird Cages and canaries."

The Bird Cage always had a little something for everyone. As one Bird Cage handbill had it:

First Appearance of Mr. Tommy Rosa, King of the Comedians and Laugh Makers. Mr. Walter Phoenix, America's Premier Song and Dance Artist. The Campbell Sisters, Serio-Comic Stars and Sketch Artists. Professor King in His Wonderful Suspension Wire Act. Mr. James Holly and Miss Lola Cory, America's Own Specialty Stars. In Addition to Our Own Great Company. Our Petite Star Miss Annie Duncan, the Tombstone Nightingale. Mr. Harry K. Morton, Comedian and End Man, in His Great Specialty, the Dublin Dancing Man. Our Serio-Comic Queen, Miss Lottie Hutchinson, in Her Selections of the Latest Gems. Mr. Neal Price, Author and Vocalist, in His Original Budget of Songs of the Day. No Advance in Prices. General Admission Twenty-five Cents. Boxes According to Location.

Following the stage acts, the theater floor would be cleared of the benches and the Bird Cage would be transformed into a regular dance hall. One of the residents of Tombstone later remembered those early morning hours: "Long about two or three o'clock, the actors got tired, and the cowboys and miners would want to dance. The chairs were stacked back and everyone danced and drank until daylight, which didn't much stop the drinkin' even after that."

On Allen Street and in other parts of Tombstone, another morning broke over the Dragoon Mountains in the east. Those miners who had not spent all night at the Bird Cage, along with a few who had, headed to their job sites, businesses, and homes. The residents of Tombstone prepared for a new day. At the Bird Cage, some ladies and other entertainers headed to their homes to rest, but others arrived to maintain the usual frenetic daytime pace. The infamous Allen Street honkytonk, as everyone knew, never closed.

CHAPTER 2

Ed Schieffelin Finds Silver in Goose Flats

I t started in the Arizona desert in 1877, in an area called Goose
Flats. A young prospector named Ed Schieffelin, wild-looking
even for the rough, itinerant fortune–seekers roaming the West,
wandered through the lands of the San Pedro Valley, his
untamed, jet-black hair and beard matted by sweat from the searing heat.
Restless, obsessive, doggedly searching for the ever-elusive ore strike, he
had left his Oregon home in 1870 on a quest.

"I can't say that I care to be rich," he had written. "If I had a fortune,
I suppose I'd not keep it long, for, now I think of it, I can't see why I
should. But I like the excitement of being right up against the earth, trying
to coax her gold away to scatter it."

Using Fort Huachuca, a new military post in southeastern Arizona, as a
base, Schieffelin, accompanied by a burro that cost him seven dollars,
searched for precious ores between the San Pedro River and the Dragoon
Mountains. In the dry washes, dusty arroyos, and rocky outcroppings, staying
out of sight of roaming Apaches, avoiding rattlesnakes, scorpions, gila

monsters, and other pests, he kept at it. Other prospectors and several of the soldiers at Fort Huachuca who knew about Schieffelin's quest began placing bets on whether he would return each night.

Fort Huachuca, after all, had only recently been established to protect settlers and travelers from the Apaches. Expert horsemen and fierce warriors, the Apaches so threatened white settlers in southern Arizona that General William Tecumseh Sherman had lamented that the United States had ever acquired the territory in the first place. As Schieffelin left one morning on his daily quest, one of the cavalry soldiers told him that he would likely find nothing in the Apache lands but his tombstone.

It was a place of strange beauty and lurking peril. Here, in this isolated desert, the infinite formations of cotton-puff clouds rolled across the bluest sky in the heavens. Standing on the smallest of heights, you could view a horizon broken only by raggy mountain ridges. This was a place where you could actually see weather march across the landscape, especially in the late afternoons when rain showers miles distant were as defined in shape as columns. Here was a place desolate and foreboding, yet quiet and peaceful.

Loading ore at a Tombstone mine. (Courtesy of the Arizona State Historical Society.)

In these western desert ranges and mountains, prehistoric peoples ten millennia back had lived in volcano-carved caves. Thousands of years before Europeans landed on the Atlantic shore, Native peoples here amidst the cactus and mesquite had adapted to the desert and knew how to accept its offerings and limitations. And now, in 1877, the land gave up another bounty—its silver.

In the early autumn of that year, the tough but as yet unsuccessful Schieffelin, nearly out of food and money, his clothes torn, arrived with ore samples at an assay office where his brother Albert worked. The rock fragments were streaked with veins of horn silver. After testing the samples and realizing the richness of the ore, the brothers returned to the site. There was more there, much more. Schieffelin had discovered one of the richest silver lodes in the history of the country. Remembering the words of the soldier at Fort Huachuca, Ed called the area the Tombstone Mining District.

Where the land yields its precious metals, the boomtown soon follows. In the quiet dignity of the desert, in the province of the jackrabbit, the rattler, and the scorpion, a crazed rush to fortune followed. About seventy miles southeast of Tucson, the town of Tombstone was built on a flat mesa, surrounded by the Whetstone, Mule, Burro, Huachuca, and Dragoon Mountains.

The western historian William Hattich wrote effusively that "The news of the fabulous Arizona strike at Tombstone spread like wildfire" and that thrilled venturers "flocked to and cast their lot with the new, exciting Golconda."

Growth followed the usual pattern in western mining boomtowns. First, the original strike attracted other miners. As the mineral lode turned out to be something approaching a bonanza, the word spread rapidly and swarms of newcomers invaded the area, clambering over the mountainsides with their burros and mining equipment. "I came to Tombstone in '81," said miner Charles Gordes, "drawn by the tales which circulated all over the west and part of the east, of fabulous riches."

Upon learning of the strike in southeast Arizona, the pattern continued as investors from other parts of the country arrived to purchase claims. Like several other entrepreneurs, a group of Boston capitalists, for example, organized the Boston and Arizona Smelting and Reduction Company in 1880. Soon familiar to southeastern Arizona Territory would be the sight of sixteen-horse teams hauling ore to stamp mills on the San Pedro River to be crushed and refined into silver bars.

With the promise of wealth and the possibility of a community came other citizens—merchants, real estate developers, horse traders, butchers, doctors, barbers, bootmakers, craftsmen, gamblers, claim jumpers, and the ubiquitous saloonkeepers. Almost with the first shovels of dirt, the saloons appeared as if obeying a fundamental law of nature.

Two days after he arrived in Tombstone by stage, a preacher named Endicott Peabody wrote: "On the outskirts were tents and the usual adobe huts and shanties." He found it much more than he expected. "The main street is long and has several two storied buildings in it and most of the others tho' small are well built—altho' they are for the most part gin mills as they call saloons here."

A visitor in late 1879 found the gin mills and also some churches but stated the obvious: "As is usually the case in mining camps the saloons are numerous and gorgeous, while the churches are small, in fact microscopically small."

Almost entirely populated by males, the town attracted gamblers and thieves and con men. It also attracted prostitutes. As the first stagecoaches carrying the joy ladies chewed into the town's new dirt roads, near riots of joy erupted.

The *Nugget* offered perorations on the majestic future awaiting this blessed southwestern Silverado. Enduring would be these veins of precious silver, as solid a foundation, the newspaper prophesied, as its encircling hills. Waxing praise upon the labors of the citizens in erecting this new community, the editors declared: "Sustained by the grandeur . . . encouraged by hopes in the future, [Tombstone] confidently steps across the threshold . . . to enter upon a new era of prosperity." John P. Clum, who would be part of the town's glory years, wrote that the "Silence of the unpeopled hills had been routed by the hum of industry."

This was the pattern, and Tombstone, Arizona, followed it. And that pattern made possible such a place as the Bird Cage Theatre.

Silver's Lure

In October 1881, John J. Gosper, acting governor of Arizona Territory, wrote a report for the Department of the Interior that described the area around Tombstone as swarming with "an army of prospectors." For Gosper, those miners and the new silver discovery that had drawn them portended a future of prosperity and fame. In a little over a year, more than three thousand locations in the Tombstone area were yielding about five hundred tons of ore daily. Here, he said, were remarkably large veins. Here, with gentle land configurations and soft and malleable soil, the ore could be extracted with few problems. Here, he said, was likely "one of the greatest mining camps ever discovered."

Across the desert they came, veteran miners from other boomtowns gone bust, buffalo hunters, teamsters, Indian fighters, real estate speculators, fortune seekers from around the country, men such as James O'Neill. A nationally famous romantic actor, visiting from San Francisco, O'Neill had recently performed as Jesus Christ in *The Passion Play* at the Grand Opera House on Mission Street. It was said that audiences were so caught up in the actor's performance that they dropped to their knees and joined the cast in prayers. But O'Neill's passions were along another line—he had silver fever.

Along with fellow actors Louis Morison and John E. Owens, O'Neill purchased shares in the Cumberland Gold and Silver Mining Company, run by a man named George M. Ciprico. The mine was not what the actors thought it was. Ciprico, a former bootblack and amateur actor, had "salted" acres of the mountainous region around Tombstone. The silver that

Tombstone in the 1880s. (Photo by Cornelius Fly; courtesy of the Arizona State Historical Society.)

O'Neill and the others discovered was the small amount placed there by Ciprico himself. Local wags later called the site "The Actors' Mine." O'Neill left Tombstone, married, and fathered a son. The boy was named Eugene.

For those who made the trek to Tombstone and for those who stayed, there were always the worries about the Apache tribesmen, led by their chief, Geronimo. With their stronghold less than eighteen miles away in the Dragoons, roving war parties were constant threats to isolated settlers and to people traveling on stagecoaches, and especially to small groups of isolated travelers. But the mesmerizing news of strikes and booms and of sudden riches drowned the fears. Tombstone's numbers kept swelling.

One of the old-timers, Charles Overlook, remembered Tombstone, and especially Allen Street, as something of a paradox—a town of many worlds but, at the same time, separated: "Desperados, gunmen, officers of the law, cowboys, miners, ladies, girls, all on one block in one of the main streets." Nevertheless, most of the outlawry and killing by the lawless elements was among themselves. They robbed each other, killed each other, and

Wells Fargo Express Company "treasure wagons" became familiar sights in new western boomtowns. (Courtesy of the Library of Congress.)

defrauded each other. Except for horse stealing, which was quite common, "No one robbed a house or molested a lady."

Over the years, of course, the legends and lore would spin helplessly out of control and the American West would be portrayed in dime novels, in newspapers and magazines, and in film and television as uncontrollably wild, with a maze of bullets constantly zinging in all directions, fired from all angles by the guns of most of its citizens. It was not like that in Tombstone or most other towns in the West, notwithstanding the torrent of yarns to the contrary.

Within two years the siren's call of the boomtown had swelled the population to over five thousand people. On wagons and stages and horses, they rode into Tombstone. Its streets were dusty and windblown and most of its buildings looked as if they had been thrown up with a total lack of architectural sense. But inside some of the establishments along Allen and Fremont Streets, it was clear that civilization had arrived. In fact, Tombstone, unlike many other boomtowns with less prospects for fabulous riches, drew an unusual number of young men and a few women who had little experience on the frontier. They were there for the chance to create new businesses or to make investments. Many had tastes refined enough to demand more than the average mining boomtown would usually offer.

Soon, Tombstone had new hotels with thick carpets, sparkling chandeliers, and soft sheets. The Cosmopolitan alone had fifty rooms, complete with bedroom furniture made of rosewood and black walnut. There were fine stores, saloons, restaurants with white-jacketed waiters and French culinary specialties, gambling halls, billiard parlors, and dance halls. F. A. Miley sold John Weiland's "celebrated San Francisco Philadelphia Lager Beer" at his Sonoma Wine House; Dillon and Kenealy's sold "Dry Goods, Fancy Goods, and Gents Furnishing Goods, all at the lowest prices"; and Carlton's Cafe, Oyster, and Chop House promised everything "first class," including ice cream for twenty-five cents.

"There are no cockroaches in my kitchen and the flour is clean," said Nellie Cashman, owner of the Russ House, whose menu on a Sunday in 1881 included such entrées as breast of lamb breaded à la mayonnaise, and chicken fricassee à la crème. As news of the silver strike reached the East, entrepreneurs, speculators, and business dealers of all kinds turned their sights to the outpost by the Dragoons. The silver strike had brought almost instant urbanity.

When Allie Earp, the wife of Virgil, later looked back on her years in Tombstone, she wrote, "Most writers seem to have the idea that Tombstone was just a cheap rawhide coco town, and that long-haired cowboys and rustlers stalked the street with a six-shooter in each hand, shooting at everything that did not suit their fancy." It was not, she said. It was a rich mining town, a community with serious, talented people.

Jennie Robertson, wife of bookseller Aleck Robertson, later told her granddaughter, "All sorts and conditions of men were going there—wild natures and others of the best in the race and culture. Some were writers, artists, professional men, lawyers and physicians."

Tombstone had the new Cochise County Court House, skillful doctors,

George Parsons, miner and diarist. (Courtesy of the Tombstone Courthouse State Historic Park.)

and five local newspapers. In Tombstone you not only could order *pinions a poulett,* and *aux Champignons* and *Salmon au Pomme 'd Terre Croquette,* but you could also find great cigars, and even take in a game of baseball.

But Tombstone also had its Whiskey Row, with such places as the Oriental Saloon, the Crystal Palace, and the Alhambra, each decorated with oil paintings, brass and mahogany bars, and fancy large mirrors, and with white-aproned bartenders skilled in mixing everything from cocktails and cobblers to flips and mashes. Allen Street beckoned to men of all tastes, refined and otherwise. Here was a scene of nightly bedlam, with cowboys often firing shots at the moon and each other, with a collection of bars and gambling joints and whorehouses nearly unmatched in the West.

Many observers of early Tombstone commented on the apparent existence of two separate societies in town. Indeed, groups of women and some men literally separated those worlds on Allen Street—certain establishments on certain stretches of the street were acceptable; most of the street was not. Where you walked and which businesses you patronized defined, to some extent, your social place.

For some, such as a young miner named James Bartee, the world of Allen Street and its infamous hangouts was a world to be shunned:

I went to work in the mines there. My wife and I both joined the Christian Church a week before we were married and have never turned from the teachings of the Bible since. Tombstone was a wild 'n woolly western town at that time—a town never could have been named more properly. Killings in the streets and saloons and gambling joints . . . besides the ones that were killed in the mines—by accident, or otherwise. I never witnessed any of the killings first mentioned, as I did not habituate such places myself, and did not hang around on the streets; if I had business to attend to at the stores, or the bank, or post office, I attended it and went home to my wife and babies, as any self-respecting man should do.

Ed Wittig Jr., age sixteen, arrived in Tombstone on July 15, 1882. "You could get out of life about anything you wanted to look for in those days," he said. "If you were looking for trouble in any form, you could find it quick; on the other hand, if you were out for a harmless good time and didn't want any trouble, you were . . . safe."

Another of Tombstone's residents in the early years, John Pleasant Gray, remembered Allen Street as a jumble of humanity, bustling, moving, exciting. "Saloons, restaurants, hotels, well-stocked stores and barber shops—all brightly lighted for those pre-electric days—kept open on both sides of Allen Street away into the night." The sounds from the dance halls and the bars, he said, "could be heard miles away by the lonely cowboy or prospector wandering in to join the gang."

And the lights and sounds of Allen Street would soon be fortified by a new establishment that, rumor had it, would be called the Bird Cage. It was now under construction at the far end of the wooden sidewalk, a few blocks from the house and studio of Cornelius Fly, the town's estimable photographer, and a certain corral soon to become notable.

CHAPTER 3

A Disturbance in Tombstone

When Wyatt Earp was a very old man, a young woman reporter asked him about the O.K. Corral incident. He said, "That fight didn't take but about 30 seconds and it seems like, in my going on 80 years, we could find some other happenings to discuss."

Tough guys get big press. Their stories fascinate—these tales of individuals less inclined to settle disputes through negotiation, more inclined to answer the primordial call to rip, tear, smite, scratch, bite, bludgeon, shoot, or dismember. In any boomtown in the West, the thugs have always been swiftly at the ready. Tombstone was in no way an exception.

In late 1881, a few weeks before completion of the new variety house at the end of Allen Street, the factional power struggles in Tombstone were at their zenith. The main provocateurs were the Earp brothers and the Clantons. Wyatt Earp, the tough lawman who had come to Tombstone looking for a fortune in silver, brought with him from Wichita and Dodge City a reputation as a cowtown cop of the "not to be messed with" variety.

Earp was also a skilled cardsharp, especially at faro, and early on he ran the Alhambra Saloon in Tombstone, a venture shared with perhaps the West's best-known ex-dentist, Doc Holliday. During his time in Tombstone, Earp owned several gambling interests.

Along with his brothers Virgil and Morgan, Wyatt and his friends opposed the forces of the Clantons, the offspring of Old Man Newman Clanton, and their friends and cohorts, not fondly known by many in those parts as the Cowboys. The name "Cowboys," in southern Arizona in the 1880s, had little to do with the professions of ranchers and drovers— the roping, branding, and trail-driving skills of ranchers and ranch hands. The term had more to do with a small group of cattle thieves and their control of money and power. From ranches in the San Pedro and San Simon Valleys, they stole cattle, especially in Mexico, ran them back into the United States, rebranded them, fought off intruders, and invaded towns and outposts in southern Arizona.

Many of them were gunslingers and misfit cowhands; some were on the run from the law. In southern Arizona, they had free rein as marauders. Tom Thornton, a hotel owner in Galeyville, Arizona, described them: "There are some who have followed the frisky longhorn herds over the Texas plains, but nine-tenths of them never saw Texas in their lives. They are wild, reckless men from all over the world. They do not claim a home, a business or close affiliation with civilization."

Through intimidation and reward, they enlisted the support of law enforcement officials and began to exercise such increasing control that federal officials back in Washington worried whether Arizona Territory would degenerate into anarchy. Although the United States Department of Justice began to provide funds to organize a corps of deputies to track down the "road agents and other criminals," the thugs and toughs in Arizona fought for control relatively unscathed. Federal posses chased the gangs back and forth across the Mexican border, arrested some, killed others, and obtained a few convictions, but the violence continued. According to estimates by deputies early in 1881, more than one hundred outlaws were operating near the Mexican border.

Early lawmen faced stiff challenges on Arizona frontier. (Courtesy of the Arizona State Historical Society.)

In November 1881, John Cooper, acting governor of Arizona Territory, writing to the U.S. marshal about the violent confrontations around Tombstone, said, "The underlying cause of the disturbances of the peace, and the taking of property unlawfully, is the fact that all men of every shade of character in that new and rapidly developed section of mineral wealth, in their mad career after money, have grossly neglected local self-government, until the more lazy and lawless elements of society have undertaken to prey upon the more industrious and honorable classes for their subsistence and gains."

Complicating the depredations of the Cowboys was the political division in the town between the forces of law and order and the press. The sheriff, Johnny Behan, and his deputies, generally siding with the Cowboy and ranching interests, did not cooperate with the U.S. marshal and his deputies, Virgil and Wyatt Earp; indeed, the sheriff and the deputies were bitter rivals. As in many parts of the frontier, federal, state, and local law enforcement officers had overlapping duties and conflicting personal ambitions that led to continual rivalries that often erupted into violence.

In Tombstone the two sides had their respective organs: the *Nugget,* which sided with Sheriff Behan, and the *Epitaph,* which sided with the Earps. A frustrated Governor Cooper lamented that the personal and political rivalries had made Tombstone a cauldron of petty divisions, making it impossible "to pursue and bring to justice that element of outlawry so largely disturbing the sense of security, and so often committing highway robbery and smaller offence."

Thirty Seconds of Reckoning

Along the boardwalk of Allen Street, the protagonists—the Cowboys and the Earp contingent—strutted and preened for their adoring sycophants and toadies and angled for power. On October 25, 1881, the so-called great showdown took place. Wyatt Earp, his brothers Virgil and Morgan, and Doc Holliday, Wyatt's misanthropic, consumptive friend with a death wish, clashed with Ike Clanton, Billy Clanton, Frank McLaury, Tom McLaury, and Billy Claiborne. Billy fled at the onset of hostilities. Billy Clanton and the McLaury brothers were killed. Virgil and Morgan Earp were both injured, but survived.

The entire infamous battle—and its immediate causes and effects—has been researched, analyzed, exaggerated, marketed, and glorified to exhaustion. It took approximately thirty seconds and the firing of about thirty shots. Books, motion pictures, television series, comic books, folk songs, and now CD-ROMs and the Internet have perpetuated the myths.

Over the years, Tombstone itself has labored to find ways to reenact and portray the great moment; papier-mâché models, have been placed where each of the shooters supposedly stood. A sign, dangling over the wooden sidewalk, once proclaimed "O.K. CORRAL—Walk where they fell!" Tourists take pictures of a wall pocked with bullet holes and of a reconstructed gibbet. A tape on a thirty-second loop explains who fired which shots. Western-garbed reenactors reeanact. Children, sporting Earp and Holliday T-shirts and twirling long-barreled rods, march the streets dreaming of things heroic.

For generations, historians and other investigators have agonized over the motives and actions of this small group of thugs. Who drew first? Who was armed and who was not? What profound utterances did Doc and Wyatt and Tom and Billy offer at the appointed time of destiny? From which direction did the shots originate? Was the whole thing orchestrated, the result of a nefarious plot?

They still argue over the character of the main protagonist, Wyatt Earp, former stagecoach driver, railroad worker, horse stealer, saloon owner, and peace officer, a man who always walked precipitously close to both sides of the law; who showed up in Tombstone with a grasping eye on silver and gambling riches; who unceremoniously dumped his second wife for the loving ministrations of an entrancing showgirl, actress, likely part-time lady of commerce, and, it is conjectured, a dancer at the Bird Cage Theatre; a man who left Tombstone a fugitive after slaughtering other tough guys in various parts of southern Arizona after his brother was killed, thus gaining the distinction of being a lawman and fugitive at the same time; who lived out the remainder of his life in the middling pursuits of gambling, racetrack betting, and prizefight refereeing; and who force-fed a lapdog biographer a mountain of misinformation and exaggeration about his life in Tombstone.

The historians continue to argue and debate. They fight it out in books and articles, in appearances at associations of writers and researchers of the West, and on the Internet. Log in to the Tombstone chat lines and argue and debate and exchange insults with a phalanx of researchers, buffs, and raconteurs.

In fact, the glorified event has been misnamed all these years. Wyatt Earp's lover, Sadie, later correctly observed that the Gunfight at the O.K. Corral could more accurately be called the "Gunfight West of Fly's House." But one of the most heavily publicized moments in U.S. history would not conjure up quite the same image with any other name. Would Henry Fonda have been quite the heroic figure on screen, battling the forces of evil, if it had been called the historic "Gunfight West of Fly's House"?

But the legends of Wyatt Earp are as old as the bullet holes west of Fly's. The literary and academic war was launched in 1931 with publication of Stuart Lake's book *Wyatt Earp: Frontier Marshal,* a heroic portrait of Tombstone's now mythic figure. It was through this book that most of the nation came to learn the story of Wyatt Earp, and it is the foundation of many of the early movie portrayals. Lake was one of several writers who worked with Earp, who died in 1929. When Fonda and other actors— Randolph Scott, Ronald Reagan, Joel McRae, James Garner, Kurt Russell, Kevin Costner, Burt Lancaster, and Hugh O'Brien—waxed heroic on the screen as Wyatt Earp, it was largely from a concoction of tall or exaggerated tales.

The Tombstone showdown has stirred powerful emotions, dividing groups of historians and history buffs, severing loose friendships. Yes, Sadie, there will be another gunfight at the O.K. Corral. It may be soon. It will be fought by historians.

Nevertheless, Glenn Boyer, one of the writers at the center of all the hullabaloo, is able to place it in perspective. He is astonished at all of the virulence, he says. After all, "Earpiana is actually a minor area of history. . . ."

Down at the end of Allen Street, just a few blocks from where all the raucousness went down, stands the Bird Cage Theatre. Like the incident near the O.K. Corral, the life of the Bird Cage now floats in a river of propositions, suppositions, and tall tales handed down. No, the Bird Cage hadn't opened by the time of the Great Occurrence, despite its depiction in some of the motion pictures. No, the greatest names in American variety entertainment did not risk venturing into arid Indian country to exhibit their genius on the boards of the Bird Cage stage. No, the blood of numerous gunslingers did not flow on the floor of the Bird Cage to mix with the cigar spit and spilled beer. No. But some wild times did take place in the famous desert nightspot. All of that is a different story.

CHAPTER 4

Playing the Desert

With word of the new Silverado, American civilization charged toward Tombstone. But Gilbert and Sullivan in the Arizona desert?

Men of the frontier longed for amusement and entertainment. In 1865, during a fifteen-week tour of frontier towns, a reporter from the East marveled at the camaraderie of many men he encountered. "Western emigration makes men larger, riper, and more fraternal," he said. Drawn together by the remoteness and shared hardships of the West, individuals formed debating societies, organized auxiliaries of Masons and the Grand Army of the Republic, and established other fraternal organizations. They welcomed any kind of diversion.

Across the West, a growing multitude of entertainers rushed to the boomtowns, hoping, like everyone else, to cash in on the new wealth, to reach these new markets. From the East and from California, song and dance artists, dancers, acting troupes, comedians, and musicians fanned out, braving rough travel conditions and primitive lodging and the threats of Indian and outlaw attacks.

Some of the entertainment came in large numbers. At the same time the Clantons and Earps were playing out the O.K. showdown, the 4-Paw's Monster Railroad Circus, Museum, Menagerie and Elevated Stage arrived at nearby Fairbank, an easy riding distance from Tombstone. In addition to twenty-five trained Shetland ponies, twenty-five trained English greyhounds, a few riding goats, a performing bear, and a den of lions, the entertainment in Fairbank included Millie Zola, Queen of the Air, who rode a bicycle on a wire fifty feet above ground. Oh yes, she was blindfolded.

In the early years of the frontier, a popular phrase for indicating that one had been around and had survived rough and rare experiences was "I have seen the elephant." The sight of elephants in the Southwest desert was indeed rare; they were part of the first circuses to hit the Southwest.

But it was not only unknown entertainers who played some of the fledgling mining and frontier towns. Some of the illustrious names of the nineteenth-century American theater played on the boards of western stages, including Edwin and Junius Booth, Harry Chapman, and Sarah Bernhardt. The traveling troupes could make healthy profits on these tours. And many of them made money on William Shakespeare.

It Wasn't Dickens

Miners, cowboys, and soldiers loved Shakespeare. From ornate theaters on the West Coast to rooms surrounded by bars and billiards, western audiences hooted and howled and shouted encouragement and insults to the actors; often they tossed coins and nuggets if they were pleased with the performance, or other more perishable products if they were not. The crowds were part of the action, sparring with the bard and his words.

On the frontier, the works of Shakespeare were not subjects of intellectual discourse but something to be wrestled with, to be brought to life, a source of rousing good times. In dance houses and bars from Denver to Sacramento, Shakespeare was turned into farce, sometimes leading to vignettes with such titles as *Hamlet and Egglet* or *Julius Sneezer*. Mountain man Jim Bridger, it was generally known, could quote long Shakespearean passages and never miss a word—and Jim Bridger, although he could speak several languages, could not read.

Westerners named mines after Shakespeare's characters, such as Ophelia and Desdemona; others named towns after Shakespeare himself, such as Shakespeare, New Mexico. A glacier in Alaska bears his name, as does a reservoir in Texas. In Calaveras County, California, Shakespearean actors performed on the stump of a giant redwood.

Some of the working men in the West became so enamored of Shakespeare that they played in amateur productions, many of them for the first time in their lives; many others simply became Shakespeare buffs, reciting long passages from the classics, reeling off obscure facts to anyone who would listen. Some of them reveled in the possibility of attaching themselves to the visiting Shakespearean troupes and signing up for bit parts.

Many individuals who had toughed out the vastness and isolation of the frontier thirsted for entertainment and some brush with culture, and they lapped up whatever came to town. But if Shakespeare had, indeed, reached the desert, theatrical critics who managed to take in some of the performances suggested that he had arrived there in pitiable shape. One historian of early California theater observed that Shakespeare's most popular creation had taken a beating: "The choice of *Hamlet* of all things, for a cast headed by two or three amateurs, may have seemed tragic indeed—unless it represented the attainment of the ludicrous in its most convulsing form."

Variety Takes the Stage

Shakespeare, indeed, made his mark in the raw towns of the West. But it would not be Shakespeare who would provide most of the entertainment; it would be the variety show. Offering a smorgasbord of entertainers whose talents came more cheaply than visiting theatrical troupes, variety shows began to draw large crowds.

Joe Bignon, Bird Cage impresario. (Courtesy of the Arizona State Historical Society.)

Across the West, in large tents, gambling halls, and makeshift auditoriums, the hoofers, singers, comics, and acrobats made their way into the more remote and wild areas of the frontier. The variety show—a series of short, diverse acts—had been part of American theater for many decades. Before the Civil War, variety shows attracted large, heterogeneous audiences, especially in New York and other major cities. But by the 1870s, with the new transportation avenues opening the West, the touring company became an increasingly popular and profitable enterprise.

A Debt to the Minstrels

Variety shows owed their origins to a number of American entertainment forms, particularly the minstrel show and burlesque. From the 1840s to the 1870s, minstrelsy was perhaps the most popular form of public amusement in the United States.

Blackfaced white entertainer Thomas "Daddy" Rice, generally known as the father of American minstrelsy, developed a song-and-dance routine around 1830 in which he impersonated an old, enfeebled black slave and dubbed him Jim Crow. The routine was wildly popular, and throughout the 1830s Rice had many imitators. The term *Jim Crow* itself would take on important social and legal implications following the Civil War.

In 1842, songwriter Daniel Decatur Emmett and a group of musicians created a program of singing and dancing in blackface to the accompaniment of bone castanets, violin, banjo, and tambourine. Calling themselves the Virginia Minstrels, they made their first public appearance in February 1843. A few years later, Edwin P. Christy's Christy Minstrels developed many of the essential features of the minstrel show.

A typical performance generally had three segments. In the first, the minstrel line, performers were seated in a semicircle. A host (the interlocutor) sat at the center, with two comedians (always called Mr. Tambo and Mr. Bones) as end men. After an opening number the interlocutor shouted,

"Gentlemen, be seated," and the end men led the ensemble in a series of songs, dances, and jokes.

The second section was the olio—miscellaneous songs and acts performed in front of a painted backdrop. It was here that each of a series of entertainers had the stage, a frenetic procession of comics, singers, dancers, and other acts, all with great exertion trying in their brief moment to stand out.

The final attraction was a one-act musical sketch, usually burlesquing a popular play or topic. These one-acts often featured two stock characters: the ever-present Jim Crow, the country bumpkin ripe for humiliation, and Zip Coon, the seemingly slick character whose self-assurance always led him to a comic comeuppance.

Most of minstrel was presented by white performers in blackface, a tradition with antecedents in the folk and ritual practices of medieval and renaissance Europe. Such a racial disguise had long allowed minstrel performers a certain social freedom to make insightful criticism of privileged persons, politicians, and institutions with impunity—to say things on stage that would normally be considered off limits. The blackface performer thus became another comic stereotype like the drunken Irishman; the cheap Scotsman; the conniving Jew; the ignorant, rural southern white, with such names as Peckerwood, Cracker, Squatter, and Hick; and other stock characters that comics performed in music halls and variety houses all over America.

Joe Bignon, later one of the central figures in the life of the Bird Cage Theatre, got his start in show business in minstrel shows, learning the routines from performers across the country. As with many of the skilled minstrel entertainers, Bignon developed his own stage identity, and sometimes dressed in wild, ragged clothes and other paraphernalia in which he bounded through acrobatic routines. Bignon, well-known on stages throughout California and Arizona, would find his niche at the Bird Cage.

Minstrel humor came from a seemingly endless run of malapropisms, non sequiturs, riddles, puns, and other word games. "Why is the letter T like an island?" the end man asks. "I don't know, Mr. Bones, why is the letter T like an island?" "Because it is in the middle of water."

From its early years in the United States, the minstrel show was often roughhouse and bawdy, almost always performed by Northern white entertainers wearing powdered burnt cork on their faces, who, when asked, often dubbed themselves "Ethiopian delineators." In early American minstrel, African American performers were originally forbidden. Nevertheless some black entertainers did secretly perform in many of the white companies. After the Civil War, mixed and all-black minstrel companies toured both America and Great Britain.

While black performers also appeared in blackface and assumed a part in the white parody of black culture, they brought their own particular talents to the stage. William "Juba" Lane was appearing with the white Georgia Champion Minstrels as early as the 1840s and presenting a unique and soon-imitated dance style.

By the 1850s, minstrel shows were using legitimate stage plays as material. One of the most popular blackface skits was an adaptation of *Uncle Tom's Cabin,* some productions of which combined minstrelsy with circus acts, using trained dogs, ponies, and in one case, a crocodile on stage. When Harriet Beecher Stowe herself was once escorted to see an adaptation of her celebrated play put on by minstrel hams and circus animals, she was unable to follow the plot. It was one of these acts that would hit the stage of the Bird Cage Theatre in 1883.

A New Kind of Burlesque

The second entertainment form that most influenced the early variety shows was burlesque. Early burlesque was satiric and comic, another entertainment form with European roots. In its American heyday, however, it bore little resemblance to earlier literary burlesques which parodied widely known works of literature, theater, or music.

The popular burlesque show of the 1870s had been transformed into a raucous affair appealing less to the intellect and more to the senses. With the arrival of Lydia Thompson and her troupe, the British Blondes, who first appeared in the United States in the 1860s, and with the advent of early "leg" shows such as *The Black Crook,* with its cast of characters such as Lulu Wontwed, Myrtle Cantwed, Stella Shantwed, and Buds, Blossoms, Lillies, Roses, Daisies, and "other little hot house plants," American burlesque began to flourish. One of the first burlesque troupes was the Rentz-Santley Novelty and Burlesque Company, created in 1870 by M. B. Leavitt, who had earlier feminized the minstrel show with her group Madame Rentz's Female Minstrels.

Although its humor and aesthetic traditions were largely derived from the minstrel show, burlesque added the important dimension of the risqué to its parodies of highbrow stage plays and other entertainment. For lonely men on the western frontier, of course, the dimension of the risqué was irresistible.

By 1880 burlesque had stormed San Francisco. The Bush Street Theatre, for example, offered a glittering array of burlesque productions with large casts of characters including Lydia Thompson's troupe in *Blue Beard;* a presentation of *The Bohemian G-Yurl and the Unapproachable Pole;* a "new grand and glittering pantomime extravaganza" entitled *Babes in the Woods;* and a less-than-highbrow *Ill Treated Il Trovatore.* Many of the cast members of these large productions on the coast eventually made their way into traveling troupes that played boomtowns across the West.

Burlesque rapidly adapted the minstrel show's three-part structure: part one composed of songs and dances rendered by a female company, interspersed with low comedy from male comedians; followed by the olio, the variety section of short specialties in which the women did not appear; and then the grand finale.

In 1869, writer William Dean Howells, lamenting the decline of artistic excellence and taste on the American stage, wrote about the emergence of burlesque: "It sets out with respecting nothing—neither taste, propriety, virtue, nor manners. Its design is to be uproariously funny and glaringly indecent." In promoting coarse fun with seductive, seminude females, burlesque, said Howells, was "low on wit, vile on jargon, and absent of manners." Although Howells was heaping ridicule on the entertainment form now gathering steam in America, his very description of it gave evidence of why it was gaining popularity, especially on the American frontier.

As the various forms of entertainment drew upon each other's practices, performers, and producers, a swirling and rich cross-fertilization came together in variety halls across the country. Like a heap of tumbleweed gathering speed and size in the Arizona desert, they would come together with special exuberance at the nightspot at the end of Tombstone's Allen Street.

Variety on the Frontier

In many of the booming western towns, some individual performers decided to stay in one location rather than rough it on the road. In the newly opened bars and saloons, with their gaudy, gilded-frame pictures, elaborate chandeliers, and great swaths of mahogany, these performers became the foundation on which variety theater proprietors built their businesses. They could draw customers with a piano player, a small stage, some singers, and dancers and then hire for short periods of time itinerant jugglers, acrobats, and other performers who would pass the hat or work for "throw money." With some gambling equipment set up for faro, roulette, monte, and poker, and most importantly, with an offering of attractive, entertaining women, these new variety halls could attract large crowds night after night.

For the customers, the smorgasbord of possibilities heightened enthusiasm. If a performer in a variety show failed miserably to satisfy or amaze, then surely the one that followed would do so. When the swilling and smoking crowds at the Bird Cage endured an especially irritating act, they were all comforted with the knowledge that the act was going to be relatively short and that it would be followed by another and then another. One of the secrets of variety's success was anticipation.

In his autobiography, the comedian Eddie Foy, one of the Bird Cage's most celebrated performers, said that writers and artists and moviemakers over the years have tried to recount the sounds and feel of entering the old western amusement halls; none of their efforts, he said, succeeded. Foy tried his best. He talked about the clatter of poker chips and dice and roulette wheels mingling with the shouts from the dealers: "Eight to one on the colors" and "Are you all down, gentlemen?" Mix in the atmosphere of the honkytonk music, the exclamations of the variety stage performers, and the sounds from the boxes overhanging the halls. Add the mutterings and shouts from the miners, soldiers, cowboys, desperadoes, and the "others more or less hard-boiled, some of them with cold steel nerves," and you had in these establishments a unique "babel of sound" filling the senses.

For those variety houses that featured "living statuary," there were young women in skintight outfits posing as Roman and Greek classical statues. Come observe "Venus Rising from the Sea" or "The Greek Slave." All of it was, of course, an early form of striptease, as many of its early adherents, armed with opera glasses, could attest.

In New York in 1875, Matt Morgan, manager of the Comique variety hall, ran afoul of the city's finest with his female tableau entitled "The Rock of Ages." When the police forced Matt to cover his living statues with a little more fabric, the local press contributed this rhyme:

> *Matt Morgan's statuary*
> *Think our police a bore*
> *Which makes each statue wary*
> *To wear a little more.*

If living statuary gave early variety-hall owners a hardly disguised excuse for displaying women's bodies in theaters, the new western halls took it many degrees further. In the 1860s a diminutive, perky entertainer named Adah Isaacs Menken blazed a trail against prudery. An unlikely combination of dramatic actress, male impersonator, and equestrienne, Adah toured the mining towns of Nevada as early as the 1860s, titillating large crowds of workers in a scanty costume that looked something like an abbreviated

Nola Forest at the Bird Cage Theatre. (Courtesy of the Arizona State Historical Society.)

Roman tunic. "She is the most undressed actress now tolerated on the American stage," said one reviewer, in no apparent fit of indignity. After taking in one of her shows in Virginia City, Mark Twain called her a "shape artist."

As variety entertainment grew more salty, as Adah imitators filled the halls, the whoops and shouts of workers filled the night air across the West. They danced the cancan and the classics, and as the howls added decibels, it was more the cancan and less the classics. A member of Duncan Clark's Female Minstrels told an interviewer, "They go crazy over a woman when they see her in tights. One of our crowd is forty-five if she is a day and as ugly as a carload of cross-eyed cats but she gets dozens of notes in every town we show in all because she wears a pair of black tights and kicks high."

The typical fare for an evening of variety entertainment included ladies chorus, song-and-dance acts, contortionists, comics, bawdy skits, and an "afterpiece" in which all the performers gathered on the stage at once for a rousing close. The variety halls also introduced an array of acrobats, roller-skaters, and other more bizarre acts.

Some establishments did try to set limits. A newspaper in El Paso complimented the owner of the Myar Opera House for excluding prostitution from the main theater area of the establishment, limiting it to the balcony. In the Park Theatre in Tucson, a newspaper reported, the usual games went on upstairs. "Here screened from observation of the curious, men of families, prominent in business and official circles, yield as readily to the wheedling caresses, naked bosoms, bare arms, shapely legs and would-be winsome smiles of the fair professionals, as does the most susceptible country guy that comes to town to sell his father's hogs."

Unlike the more conventional theatrical offerings, variety shows were stag affairs. In this atmosphere of alcohol, gambling tables, and scantily dressed, willing women, the variety theaters were designed to induce men to turn over to the establishment as much of their fortunes as possible. The variety shows were the forerunners of the one-stop, Las Vegas–style casinos. A century later in Las Vegas, the inducements would be veritable kingdoms and palaces—the Taj Mahal, or a miniature city of New York—where gambling, booze, sex, and entertainment, all in one magical place, reach their grasping tentacles into patrons' pockets. The first variety shows that began to appear in towns across the West were different in scale but not in concept.

American variety theaters were quite similar to music halls in Victorian Britain. In 1875 there were over three hundred of them in London alone with names like The Empire and The Hippodrome. They were essentially pubs with a stage featuring singers, dancers, magicians, and other specialty acts that would vie for attention and, in some cases, survival amidst the din of tipsy audiences free to cheer or insult the entertainment. Although the British temperance movement led to the establishment of a few liquor-free music halls in the waning years of the nineteenth century, music halls remained popular through World War II.

By the mid-1800s, variety was America's most common form of popular stage entertainment. Usually presented in makeshift locations such as converted saloons or abandoned warehouses, variety halls or "museums" always featured a bar and were usually so shabby that performers often called them "dumps" or "honkytonks." The audiences were as unruly as the shows, with fevered boos and hisses, frequent brawls, and rudeness raised to an art form.

One typical variety song, "Such a Delicate Duck," laments a courting failure in a potato patch. By Victorian-era standards, the ditty was somewhat lewd:

> *I took her out one night for a walk,*
> *We indulged in all sorts of pleasantry and talk.*
> *We came to a potato patch, she wouldn't go across;*
> *The potatoes had eyes and she didn't wear no drawers!*

The New York *Spirit of the Times* described the variety business as "music by the band, farce, beautiful ballads, performances of dogs and monkeys, stump oratory, character songs and dances, negroisms, Dutchisms, ballet, gymnastic feats and burlesque. . . . Blondes are in the majority and some of them very pretty."

Theaters such as the Comique in Dodge City, the McDaniels in Cheyenne, and the Cricket in Denver offered extraordinary billings of entertainers. They worked for short periods charming the locals. When their acts became old to the limited number of townspeople, they headed out on the stagecoach for the next cow town or mining camp, later to return to new audiences when the population of the town they had just left changed after a year or two.

A writer for the *Idaho Statesman* seemed amazed by the wonders of modern diversion that had risen in an early mining camp: "There were hurdy-gurdies and variety halls running full blast, and some theatres or halls where one may witness a full length play for the sum of one dollar from the gallery or two dollars from the main floor." Playing tonight, the Healey Brothers, including "Grotesque Dancing, Leg Mania and Contortion Feats in which they stand positively alone. In their specialty The Happy Hottentots. P.S. These gentlemen are the highest kickers in the universe—bar none."

In 1878, a rotund, jovial German named Alexander Levin erected a large building in Tucson, Arizona, called Levin's Opera House that began to offer the same kind of variety fare he had witnessed on the West Coast. Levin said that his place was "something similar to the Tivoli in San Francisco," where the hostesses were clad in short blue skirts, black silk stockings, and low-necked blouses. Levin's Opera House was the Arizona forerunner of the Bird Cage Theatre.

One of the most spectacular presentations in the variety theaters, a novelty that drew special exuberance and grateful gasps from the tough mining audiences, was the flying trapeze. Appropriated from beer gardens and brothels, the device was used by athletic young women to swing above the crowds, sometimes removing articles of clothing in midair. Some of the variety halls used swings; others rigged up a rope from which the performer would glide from one side of the upper rafters to the other.

Mrs. Frank Leslie, wife of the publisher of *Leslie's Weekly*, one of the nation's most influential periodicals, described a night at a Cheyenne,

Wyoming, theater in 1877. The theater, she said, was narrow, like a long box rather than a horseshoe, so that the audience on the side could almost shake hands with the audience on the other. "The trapezes through which the wonder Mlle. Somebody is flying and frisking like a bird, are all swung from the stage to the back of the house, so that her silken tights and spangles whisk past within a hand's breadth of the admiring, who can exchange civilities, or even confidences with her in her aerial flight."

At the Bird Cage, the Mlle. Somebody was Lizette, the Flying Nymph. Just as Mrs. Leslie remembered the high-wire entertainer in the honkytonk in Cheyenne, thousands of Bird Cage patrons over the years never forgot the sight of Lizette.

This one kind of show production symbolized everything in variety entertainment that drew in larger and larger crowds of miners, cowboys, and soldiers—both the mature and the barely shaven. It had elements of the circus and girlie shows; it had a blend of the sensuous and the daredevil; it was rough and tumble in areas of the country where men gambled, looked for the quick strike, and sought respite from the routine.

CHAPTER 5

Booming Culture in the Boomtown

F or the new residents of Tombstone, the magnificent silver lode and its riches allowed the accumulation of culture to keep pace with the accumulation of wealth. Everything boomed. When Clara Spalding Brown came to Tombstone with her husband, Theodore Brown, in 1880, she lamented the cultural and social abyss into which she had been plunged. "The only attractive places visible are the liquor and gambling saloons," she wrote. "The ladies of Tombstone are not so liberally provided with entertainment, and find little enjoyment aside from a stroll about town after sunset, the only comfortable time of the day."

In the spring of 1880, Tombstone held a fair to benefit the local church, and the only place that afforded sufficient room was a middling-size auditorium with an adjacent dance hall and bar. A reporter for the *Tucson Weekly Citizen* noted that, "Ordinarily, the bare association of such a place, with a church charity, would cause all the prayer books in the district to rattle with indignation." Nevertheless, the fair's managers, realizing that the needs outweighed the moral reservations, proceeded. Everything went well until the dance house began to get warmed up, when calls such as "hoof it to the left," "hug the gals on the corner," "hoop 'em down the middle," "mule punchers to the right," and "all hands chase to the bar" shocked some of the fairgoers. Although the benefit was a success, the reporter was confident that the next church fair would not take place in the same location.

As the town filled with doctors, barbers, store owners, lawyers, and other new citizens and their families, and as Tombstone welcomed all the accoutrements of a growing society, the thirst for recreation and entertainment and especially the theater intensified. Soon, Clara Brown would see more in Tombstone than saloons, adobe shacks, and acres of dirt.

Within three years of Ed Schieffelin's strike, with Tombstone boasting a telegraph system, restaurants with elaborate fixtures and chandeliers and tableware, shops with the latest fashions from the West Coast, and the beginnings of a school system, a lawyer named Wells Spicer noted wryly in early 1880 that culture was also on the horizon: "The town is not altogether lost, even if there is a population of 1,500 people, with two dance houses, a dozen gambling places, over twenty saloons and more than five hundred gamblers. Still, there is hope; for I know of two bibles in town. . . ." Spicer could have also included dancing schools, a library club where subscribers gathered to read the latest literature, and a musical society. A resident of Tombstone later recalled that the musical society "once put on an opera to help raise funds for the construction of a church. Although they had to send to San Francisco for costumes, which proved exceedingly expensive, yet they cleared several hundred dollars for their project."

There was also a dramatic society. John Clum, Indian agent, mayor of Tombstone, and founder of the *Tombstone Epitaph,* was one of the principal founders of the Tombstone Amateur Dramatic Club. He later remembered performing in a production of *The Toddles,* an effort that "netted about $120, which is quite an addition to the cemetery fund." Some of the amateur efforts were disappointing. A note in a local paper reported that one

Thomas Vincent, director of the Tombstone Cornet Band. (Courtesy of the Tombstone Courthouse State Historic Park.)

attempt to organize an acting troupe had been downright embarrassing: "When any one of the proposed company commenced to sing all the others began to weep."

But the locals were undeterred. In November 1880, a group of Tombstone residents put on the greasepaint and performed a play called *Andy Blake, or The Irish Diamond,* followed by a concert and ball. The proceeds went to the Catholic church and the town hospital.

And, while visiting Tombstone, a reporter for Tucson's *Star,* unaware of some of the fine amateur work being done in Tombstone, bemusedly noted that "Shakespeare's ghost is prowling about this argentiferous graveyard. They have organized a dramatic association here."

Professional variety troupes also began to visit the new town. After Billy Brewster's Minstrels performed in a makeshift auditorium, the *Star* reported that the group was "elated at the great activity in the district," with many new adobe buildings being erected. Billy Brewster looked forward to returning.

Dick Deadeye and Little Buttercup in Silverado

In 1879, Gilbert and Sullivan's *H.M.S. Pinafore* hit the desert like a magisterial dust-devil. The masterpiece comic opera, music by Sir Arthur Sullivan, text by W. S. Gilbert, was first produced at the Opera Comique, London, on May 28, 1878. Less than a year later it was in the American West, opening in San Francisco's new Tivoli Opera House. *Pinafore* played to full houses for sixty-three consecutive nights, and over the next twenty-five years, the Tivoli stock company presented more than four thousand performances.

A bouncy, quaint melodrama about British seafarers, it was packed with romance, laughs, and to those who understood its targets, searing parody. *Pinafore* soon became one of the most popular hits on American stages.

Folks who liked good old-fashioned patriotic melodies cheered along with those who enjoyed mocking good old-fashioned patriotic melodies. It satirized things nautical and, at the same time, charmed those who liked things nautical. The production could be whatever its audience wished it to be. Across the country, aspiring stage performers practiced the new dance craze, the sailor's hornpipe.

On the quarterdeck of the *Pinafore* romped Rt. Hon. Sir Joseph Porter, K.C.B, First Lord of the Admiralty; Captain Corcoran, commander of the *Pinafore;* seamen Ralph Rackstraw and the foul, ugly Dick Deadeye; Josephine, the captain's daughter; and Little Buttercup, a Portsmouth bumboat woman and "reddest beauty of all Spithead."

Ralph is in love with the captain's daughter, Josephine. She, however, is to be betrothed to Sir Joseph Porter, who arrives attended by his sisters, cousins, and aunts. In the meantime, Ralph plans to elope with Josephine, the crew assisting. The plot is overheard by Dick Deadeye. Alone on the deck, Captain Corcoran sings to the moon. Little Buttercup moves in, declaring her affection. The captain says that because of his rank he can only be her friend, but she mysteriously replies that "things are seldom what they seem." And so on and so on.

In this story of a naval captain's daughter who prefers a common sailor to the First Lord of the Admiralty, the authors spoofed Victorian social stratification and turned out memorable songs. In "When I Was a Lad," The First Lord explains how to attain his lofty position:

> *Now landsmen all, whoever you may be,*
> *If you want to rise to the top of the tree,*
> *If your soul isn't fettered to an office stool,*
> *Be careful to be guided by this golden rule—*
> *Stick close to your desks and never go to sea,*
> *And you all may be rulers of the Queen's Navee!*

When *Pinafore* premiered in the United States, it became an immediate sensation. *Pinafore* mania swept the nation. Unauthorized companies performed it all over the country, and several competing troupes played it simultaneously to packed houses in New York. When the composers brought their own D'Oyly Carte company over in 1879, it only made matters worse. The songs were played and sung everywhere, and the line "What never? Well . . . hardly ever" became part of everyday conversation. One newspaper editor angrily commanded his reporters to never use the phrase again, only to have them respond as a group, "What never?" Defeated, he said, "Well, hardly ever!"

In September 1879, George N. Pring of San Francisco traveled to Tucson to scout out the opportunities to bring theater to the desert. Pring took the railroad, which was then under construction as far as Casa Grande, and then a stage to Tucson "with a view of bringing here a first class opera dramatic troupe, selected from the best talent of San Francisco, including the well-known actress, Pauline Markham." On November 3, 1879, Pring's troupe presented *H.M.S. Pinafore* and then in the weeks following, such productions as *Trial by Jury* and *The Rose of Auvergne*.

While in Tucson, Pring gave up management of the company and the new directors changed its name to the English Opera Company. In December 1879, the ship *Pinafore* sailed into Tombstone for a one-week engagement in a barely adequate makeshift auditorium. The production was called *Pinafore on Wheels,* and its cast included several beautiful women. Adorned in their elaborate costumes, performing against a backdrop of impressive sets, the troupe was a welcome sight for Tombstone residents. The westerners would now cheer on the likes of Captain Corcoran, Little Buttercup, and Dick Deadeye. Thus an English satire on various institutions and authorities of the day became a vehicle of entertainment for groups of American mine workers, gamblers, and ranchers, which the creators, Mr. Gilbert and Mr. Sullivan, undoubtedly never had in mind.

The cast included a gorgeous young performer going by the name of May Bell, who played a character known as Cousin Hebe. May Bell was actually a stagestruck eighteen-year-old from San Francisco named

Nellie Boyd, star of the first professional troupe to play in Tombstone, November 1880. (Courtesy of the Tombstone Courthouse State Historic Park.)

Josephine Sarah Marcus, and she would be of special interest to two prominent Tombstone figures—Sheriff Johnny Behan and Deputy Marshal Wyatt Earp.

From Santa Barbara to San Bernardino, south to Prescott, and on to Tucson and Tombstone, the troupe had traveled, first by train, and then in two stagecoaches and a large transport wagon to carry the stage props and luggage. Grinding along a trail that spit up dust with each revolution of the wheels, through isolated desert outposts made of thick adobe, they heard rumors of Apaches on the attack and worried about breaking down in the rough terrain. The frilly costumes and other elaborate paraphernalia for *H.M.S. Pinafore* must have seemed in this desolate setting to be from another galaxy.

New Cathedrals of Entertainment

In 1879 the blackface dancer and entertainer Joe Bignon opened the Theatre Comique in Tombstone. The following year, other entrepreneurs followed Bignon's lead and built several theaters to compete with it. The Sixth Street Opera House, formally the E. Fontana Dance Hall, appeared just below the southwest corner of Fremont and Sixth, near the later site of the Bird Cage Theatre; it was co-managed by William J. "Billy" Hutchinson, a variety performer. There was Danner & Owens Hall, an auditorium on Allen Street that had modern footlights and elaborate chandeliers; Ritchie's Hall, a building on Fifth Street, used not only for theater troupes but for union meetings; and Turn-Verein Hall, at the corner of Fourth and Fremont Streets, also used for dances, meetings, and traveling theater groups. These were relatively small buildings.

As they worked the Fontana Dance Hall, Billy Hutchinson and his wife, Lottie, also an accomplished theatrical performer, saw that the growing town had a need for something much more spectacular than the Fontana or Ritchie's Hall. The Hutchinsons dreamed of their own major variety theater, a place that would attract performers from all over the country. From their experiences on the road and during these early days of Tombstone came their visions of the Bird Cage Theatre.

In the spring of 1880, the Star Novelty Troupe, one of the first entertainment companies to travel the newly completed tracks to Tucson, took the unpaved roads to Tombstone for an engagement. The troupe brought with it "Ethiopian Specialties" by Robert Scott, German songs and funny sayings by David Boothby, one-man-band Professor Singer, recitations by F. E. Brooks, and Patti Rosa's clog dancing. Such variety entertainers would flock to Tombstone in the coming years.

In November 1880, Tombstone welcomed the nationally known actress Nellie Boyd. She had made her New York debut five years earlier as Ned Compo in the Booth's Theatre production of *Flying Scud*. This was her first sojourn in the Southwest; indeed, it was the first time an established performer from the East had ventured into the Arizona desert. Before the Arizona trip, she told a reporter that the thought of meeting hostile Indians had made her uneasy. Nevertheless, her Nellie Boyd Dramatic Company trooped into Tombstone's cramped Ritchie's Hall to perform *Fanchon the Cricket* and *The Banker's Daughter* by Bronson Howard, and a number of other productions, all of which required a substantial cast and much prop work. The enterprising Miss Boyd and her company persevered to much acclaim. These were the first of many performances by professional traveling stage companies in Tombstone, and they opened for the infant town a sizable cultural door.

When Boyd and other well-known actresses performed in the exploding boomtown in southeastern Arizona, the crowds packed the small halls night after night. After an appearance by Miss Jeffrey-Lewis in the play *Forget-Me-Not*, the *Tombstone Epitaph* almost chided the acting company for fearing an empty hall: "There was a very large house which was quite an agreeable surprise to the company. So fearful were they that they had almost decided to give Tombstone the go-by."

But even with the talented touring companies now heading for Tombstone, some of the individual acts were as rough as the mesquite.

Schieffelin Hall. (Courtesy of the Tombstone Courthouse State Historic Park.)

Meet Pearl Ardine, jig dancer. Pearl could swoop to the floor in the middle of her routine, snatch bills thrown on the stage, and stuff them in her stockings with unmatched athleticism. The hard-rock miners of Tombstone flocked to see Pearl.

In early 1881, the professional actor Robert McWade, who had played alongside such performers as Edwin Booth and Lotta Crabtree, came to Tombstone to perform his highly regarded version of *Rip Van Winkle* at the Sixth Street Opera House. To accommodate the appearance of McWade, the management ripped up the bar and stove and removed other items to make room for 150 seats. Professional touring groups needed larger facilities.

Tombstone's Great Theatrical Edifice

In the early months of 1881, construction began on a theater that would attract entertainers from around the country. Al Schieffelin, brother of the man whose silver discovery had started Tombstone, Ed Schieffelin, built at the corner of Fremont and Fourth Streets a massive, two-story adobe structure with a stage that rivaled, at least in size, the great theatrical edifices on Broadway and in San Francisco. The place was 130 feet long with a ceiling of 24 feet and seating capacity of seven hundred. It had a 40-foot-wide stage with a magnificent drop curtain depicting an outdoor scene. For the theater boosters in Tombstone, the completion of the great hall was a day for huzzahs and hallelujahs. It would not be a variety theater in the mold envisioned by the Hutchinsons for the Bird Cage, but it would be a place where those in Tombstone who sought culture could find it.

In early 1881, Schieffelin Hall neared completion. The *Epitaph* reported: "It is now a pile of dry mud two stories high, with numerous openings for doors and windows. When the cornice is on, windows in, doors etc. completed, and the ugly ash-colored mud hidden beneath an exterior of mastic, in imitation of brick or stone, it will be quite another affair." The building, declared the editorialist, will fill an enormous, long-felt community need.

It was not gaudy or decorative; it was functional. But here was a place, when packed with audiences, that could give real meaning to the term "full house." Schieffelin Hall was inaugurated on March 17, 1881, with an Irish League Ball. It was, of course, St. Patrick's Day.

Destination: Tombstone

In the late summer of 1881, W. A. Cuddy, an experienced actor and promoter, organized the Tombstone Dramatic Relief Association, and on September 15, 1881, the association mounted its first serious theatrical presentation at Schieffelin Hall, Tom Taylor's five-act drama *The Ticket-of-Leave Man*. Proceeds from the play were used to purchase a fire alarm bell for the Rescue Hook and Ladder Company. A writer for the *Daily Nugget* lauded the performance as "in many respects far above that usually given by amateurs" and especially heralded the work of Lottie

Hutchinson, who "did very well in her character songs, winning much applause."

The amateur actors and actresses of Tombstone kept all of the town's stages busy. So actively did the groups promote their plays, so dedicated was their work, that amateur groups from Tucson and other communities in southern Arizona arrived in Tombstone to see their work and also to participate in it. Occasionally the Tombstone Dramatic Relief Association even went on the road, boarding stages and hauling wagons to Tucson to give performances.

The preoccupation of theatergoers and artists continued to be *Pinafore*. George Whitwell Parsons, who kept a daily journal of his life in Tombstone during the 1880s, saw a production in 1882: "*Pinafore* good tonight and much enjoyed by immense house. [Fred] Brooks especially fine an Admiral. I used to admire him at Tivoli in San Francisco as that character. Ed Suman also very good as Dick Deadeye." John Clum, who was part of the chorus of Jolly Jack Tars, agreed. "The amateur talent of Tombstone produced opera as well as drama, and the rendition of *Pinafore* by our local troupe was fully equal to any professional performance I have ever witnessed." Social life in Tombstone from Clum's perspective equaled even the communities in "the effete East."

Here in this ruggedly serene location in southeastern territorial Arizona, smack up against hostile Apache Indians still making guerrilla attacks and then disappearing into the craggy rock formations of the Chiricahua Mountains, more than sixty miles from any town that bore any semblance of modern American civilization, lacking immediate accessibility from the growing railroad system webbing across the West; here, suddenly, because of silver, was everyone from Nellie Boyd to the offbeat entertainer Mlle. De Granville, a female weightlifter.

Back in San Francisco, entertainers and booking agents began to hear of Tombstone. M. B. Leavitt and Al Hayman, managers of San Francisco's Bush Street Theatre, decided that all the attractions under their engagement in San Francisco from the East should return over the Southern Pacific

Railroad and, with stagecoach service to some locations, play theaters in Los Angeles, San Bernardino, Tucson, Tombstone, Santa Fe, Las Vegas, Albuquerque, Trinidad (Colorado), Denver, and Kansas City. The side trip to Tombstone meant a wild fifty-mile stage ride from Benson, Arizona.

Traveling companies that were already crisscrossing the country, hitting boomtowns from Butte to Virginia City, began to alter their routes to check out the wild town in the desert whose potential as a show place suddenly seemed on fire. Tombstone in the 1880s thus became a popular stop for variety troupes, especially as they made their way to and from the West Coast.

Some entertainers traveled alone or with one or two partners. They laid out their own plans, booking with stage managers in advance. Finding work, anticipating travel schedules, and dealing with unanticipated problems was tricky and uncertain for the itinerant stage entertainers, especially as they ventured into places as isolated as Tombstone. But the word got around the circuits that the infant boomtown in southeastern Arizona was a hot place in more than temperature.

It even had a local humorist. John P. Clum—Indian agent, newspaper editor, and thespian, among many occupations—who used Schieffelin Hall to recite his own poetic creation:

The play that evening was Macbeth,
And Uncle Josh with bated breath
Had watched with eyes amazed and keen
Until the famed sleep-walking scene,
When Lady Macbeth strives to blot
From her stained hands the damned spot.
And as she washed them in the air
And cried out at the blood still there,
Then Uncle Josh asked one near by,
"What makes that woman swear an' cry
And wring her hands an' go on so?
What's on 'em I'd jes like to know?"

"It's Duncan's blood," the man replied,
"She strives the fearful stains to hide."
"Why don't she wash her hands, b'gosh,
With Ivory Soap?" quoth Uncle Josh!

Tombstone now had its large hall to house major performances of legitimate theater. It also had organized amateur clubs and associations and a citizenry eager to perform. It had a growing population of miners thirsting for more entertainment, a different kind of entertainment. It did not have a variety theater. But one was on the way.

CHAPTER 6

The Honkytonk of Allen Street

A
t the corner of Allen Street and Sixth, not far from the O.K. Corral at the time of the celebrated showdown, workers were putting the finishing touches on an adobe building that would become the Bird Cage Theatre. Like other amusements and attractions of the growing Silverado in the desert, the Bird Cage would be inspired by the West's greatest mining metropolis: San Francisco.

"As good as San Francisco" became the most popular advertising slogan. Tombstone was to be the new oasis of Bay City culture, a place where the whiskey, the food, the theater, and all the other creature enjoyments could flow from the silver wealth of its surrounding hills and mountains. The Tombstone Dining Room's menu boasted that any kind of food or liquor that could be found in San Francisco could be found there, guaranteed by the proprietor, Charles Kreuder. Want a tenderloin or a Champagne Cognac? It was all there at the Tombstone Dining Room. What Tombstone needed now was a variety theater just as spectacular as any in San Francisco.

67

In July 1881, Sixth Street Opera House manager Billy Hutchinson and his wife, Lottie, paid six hundred dollars for a plot of land at the southeast end of Tombstone's Allen Street. Hutchinson's dream, at least at the beginning, was to build a theater in which respectable citizens might feel at home. Hutchinson had ties with a San Francisco liquor firm named Schruff-McCrumb and it was through that business arrangement that Billy secured the funds to erect his building.

As the time approached for the opening of the new theater, Billy was in San Francisco recruiting talent for his enterprise. Through Billy and Lottie's show-business connections and some enthusiastic salesmanship, the duo managed to persuade enough frustrated actors, dancers, gagsters, and other entertainers to dump their San Francisco dreams of success temporarily in the Bay and head for the desert. A new entertainment mecca would arise in the middle of rattlers, tumbleweeds, and bands of Apaches.

Christmas in Tombstone, 1881. Madame DuPree, a "renowned pedestrienne," handily defeated three of the town's fittest women in a walking match. The *Epitaph* reported that the champion walker, once nearly an invalid, had achieved nearly perfect fitness through living and eating according to nature's strictures.

At Schieffelin Hall, Santa Claus descended from the heavens, or at least from the building's upper beams, to distribute gifts to more than 250 children. At the Rockaway Oyster House, the chefs served up roast turkey, suckling pig, veal, sheep and, of course, the oysters. The freshness of the oysters, imported from as far away as Baltimore, was somewhat questionable.

Amidst the holiday cheer and goodwill, the mini-war between the Earps and Clantons following the shootout escalated into ominous rumors of assassination. The mayor, a judge, and others, it was said, might not survive the year.

But at 517 Allen Street, all those fears and trepidations were swept momentarily out of mind. The *Epitaph* reported: "The Bird Cage Theatre on Allen Street near Sixth will be dedicated by Hutchinson's Variety troupe in an entirely new and original series of plays, songs, dances, etc. that will serve to interest and amuse the audience."

A few days before the opening, Hutchinson assembled his new variety troupe for a performance at Schieffelin Hall to a crowded, boisterous throng who had paid the one-dollar admission. Although Lottie Hutchinson was not in particularly good voice, stricken by a severe cold, the exuberant show went on. One comic number was so funny, according to a reporter, that tears rolled down the cheeks of many in the audience. The winsome female entertainment, featuring several young songstresses, gave the troupe a fresh, slightly mischievous atmosphere from that first night on stage.

> Burns and Trayers as end men proved themselves of no small ability in their line and kept the audience convulsed with laughter while listening to their original jokes and comic songs. Miss Irene Baker ingratiated herself at once into the good graces of the house, as well as being pretty, she has a sweet and cultivated voice and is a clever actress. . . . Harry Lorraine's piccolo solo was deservedly well received. . . . the after-piece, entitled "The Ashbox Inspector," was side-splitting. . . .

The Bird Cage troupe was ready.

The Inauguration

On December 26, lines of miners, alkali-dusted cowboys, and storekeepers laid down their fifty cents and scrambled inside the new theater. For the Bird Cage opening, Billy spiced the place with several young dancers.

From its first days, the Bird Cage was a sensation. The January 4, 1882, *Epitaph* talked about the gas-fired jets that bathed the stage in light. In the cramped, boxlike adobe structure, day-wage miners and assorted drifters and droolers gathered nightly, each perfectly willing to collapse into a guzzle-and-holler frenzy at the sight of the winking chorus girls parading before them. The hostesses in their short skirts and low necks flitted about, encouraging customers to drink better-quality brands and more of it. They were instant friends to the miners and other clientele whose need for such friends seemed to grow once inside the establishment.

One of the first leading attractions at the Bird Cage was Mlle. De Granville, described in the *Daily Nugget* as "the great female Hercules, in her marvelous feats of strength." Known as "the woman with the iron jaw," Mlle. De Granville's special talent was picking up heavy objects with her teeth. The noted stage performer was a veteran in the West, a hardened trouper, who had braved such places as Colorado's Mountaineer Hall, an entertainment temple consisting mostly of wooden boards wedged into a mountain-side for a stage, with hanging bedsheets for dressing rooms and a crate for a box office. When you have conquered Mountaineer Hall, the Bird Cage hardly offered a challenge.

Along with the esteemed female power lifter, Billy had managed to secure the services of the Irish comic duo of Burns and Trayers, a comic singer named Irene Baker, and Carrie Delmar, a serious opera singer.

Like other variety theaters, the Bird Cage was a maze of temptations, a model layout from which management could extract as much lucre as possible from its clientele. Men were led past the bar, through the gambling

Prospector in front of the Bird Cage Theatre. (Courtesy of the Arizona State Historical Society.)

area, and then into the main hall with its stage. For the thirsty, the greedy, the lusty, or even those interested merely in stage entertainment, the Bird Cage offered its delights. It was a tantalizing route which few diversion-starved men could resist.

It shared certain characteristics, not altogether classy, with other raucous variety halls in mining towns across the West. When the wife of a doctor wandered into one of California's variety halls, she was taken aback—not by the dancers or the droolers but by the floor. The tobacco juice was so abundant on the hardwood floor, she complained, that she risked drowning. "Luckily the floor was uneven and it lay around in puddles, which with care one could avoid."

For twenty-four hours a day, the Bird Cage never closed its doors. The Hutchinsons moved new entertainers onto the Bird Cage stage with the speed necessary to satisfy an increasingly demanding public appetite. "We were not particular to the extremes," remembered a resident of Tombstone in the 1880s, "but we were fair to middling keen on getting a real show."

The Hutchinsons, using connections they had made through their acting careers, brought in an increasing number of quality variety acts. A reporter for the *Star* said after a visit to the Bird Cage that a "person can spend several hours in an enjoyable manner by visiting this already notorious variety theater. Billy Hutchinson, the manager, adds new talent almost daily, and the house today stands peer over any south of San Francisco for elegant, beautiful, and accomplished artists. Among the actors and actresses are Tom Rosa, an old San Francisco favorite; Jim and Lola Holly, Ed and Nola Forest, Pearl Ardine, Irene Osturn, and several others."

When Billy traveled to San Francisco to select talent to grace the boards of his little theater, he never went in vain. Whenever the stagecoach rolled into Tombstone carrying new performers for the Bird Cage or other establishments, groups of men gathered—scores of miners, cattle rustlers, and tradesmen, all trying to catch glimpses of the passengers who were descending from the coach. A chorus of "ohs" and whistles always greeted the performers, who coyly held their full skirts as they stepped down.

"The pink of perfection," Billy would say of a new entertainer, "Miss Kitty Mountain, who has established herself at once as a favorite." Or: "The pet of the boys, Little Pearl, who has many imitators but no equal."

Billy tried everything. He had masquerade balls in which the local clientele would mingle with the entertainers—all dressed in the most outrageous attire available. Through the establishment he paraded offbeat comics, raunchy ballad singers, and women who impersonated men and vice versa. It gave comic entertainers such as David Waters and Will Curlew a change to parade their most outrageous attire.

The *Nugget* claimed that by February 1882 the Bird Cage was offering variety shows second to none on the Pacific Coast and expected to get even better. "As new specialties are constantly being added, its popularity is sure to increase with each succeeding week. . . . The attractions now being offered at the Bird Cage Theatre are second to no variety show on the coast."

For Billy Hutchinson, who had admired San Francisco's variety theaters, and had recruited Bay talent for his enterprise, this was the ultimate compliment. Here, amidst the sagebrush and the mountains, he had created a honkytonk that drew the ultimate comparisons.

John Pleasant Gray, a young graduate of the University of California, Berkeley, in 1880, joined his parents in Tombstone soon after graduation. Sixty years later, he remembered his impressions of those first days he spent in the Arizona boomtown and its frenetic energy and excitement. He remembered the mix of humanity rushing about at a constantly furious pace, especially on Allen Street, with its array of saloons and restaurants, all brightly lit, and the music and roar of the crowds from the saloons and gambling parlors, the shouts of "Promenade to the bar" at some dance hall, or a yell of "Keno" from a winning player, and occasionally some gunshots on the streets.

But actual crime and violence, he said, were not as prevalent as the wild atmosphere might have suggested. "You could sleep in the midst of this," he wrote, "if you could simply consider it as harmless as the noise of a boiler

David Waters dressed for a masquerade ball. (Courtesy of the Tombstone Courthouse State Historic Park.)

factory—and as to danger from holdup men, even the name itself was unknown. A man's roll was perfectly safe unless he spent it of his own will."

Rosa Schuster, whose house was close to the Bird Cage, agreed with Gray to a certain extent. "No," she said, "Tombstone was never a really tough camp as some people seem to think . . . . Of course a lot of bad men came here at different times who would pirouette around with a gun in their hand and act the bully for a while. But sooner or later there always cropped up someone a mite faster, who would eventually down the first bad actor, and, in turn, be downed by a faster man later. And so on and so on, ad infinitum. . . . Boothill got them all in due time, so you see we were a well conducted camp."

For a brief time following the O.K. Corral shootout, the huge crowds congregating in and around the Bird Cage worried law enforcement officials. William Breakenridge, who worked for Sheriff Behan, later remembered patrolling the Bird Cage for possible trouble between the Earps and the Clantons and their cronies. "It was a great resort for both factions," he said, "and the bar did a rushing business. Although no one had been killed there, and Hutchinson ran it in an orderly manner, we looked for trouble between the two factions to come off at anytime." It was during one of his nightly canvassings of the Bird Cage area that Breakenridge saw gunslinger Frank Stillwell lurking in the shadows, pistol drawn. Stillwell was apparently looking for Doc Holliday, and Breakenridge later boasted that he had thwarted an assassination.

When the Hutchinsons first opened the Bird Cage, they ostensibly had in mind a marginally respectable entertainment spot that would draw interest from most segments of Tombstone society. How they expected to achieve that goal with the brothel element an integral part of the establishment is open to speculation. Nevertheless, the proprietors tried. Billy and Lottie instituted Ladies Night—all ladies admitted free. But the whole thing seemed to be more of a dare than an inducement.

Nevertheless, Beatrice Leo, who played the Bird Cage when she was about seventeen years old in 1882, looked back on her own experience fondly.

"I was very green and did not know as much of the life. But [I] know that there were girls to sell drinks and made good money, for they got twenty cents on a bottle of beer which cost one dollar, and they did sell lots. The performers were not obliged to go in the boxes, as they were called. . . ."

Whatever the intent and inclinations of the Hutchinsons, what they had at the end of Allen Street was a place that followed the sage thinkings of successful entrepreneurs from centuries past—know thy customers, give them a quality product in short supply, and cater to their needs with flair and inspiration. And give them a sense that they are getting something unavailable at other establishments and, particularly in the frontier West, slightly forbidden.

The Soiled Doves

T hey called them many names on the western frontier: chippies, ladies of joy, nymphs, shady ladies, sporting girls, and soiled doves. A. H. Noon, a reporter from Chicago on an early visit to Tombstone, described numerous saloons and cribs where prostitutes catered to the male boomtown society. Most of the women, he said, were homely and forlorn, a "ghastly picture of [a] Low Type of Immorality." In the Bird Cage it was different. This was a higher class of immorality.

As word of boomtowns like Tombstone spread in the West, usually the first women to arrive in remote regions were dance-hall girls and prostitutes. In Tombstone they arrived in great numbers.

In variety halls across the country, some actresses, dancers, and other performers supplemented their incomes. Some theaters featured a "green room" where part of the cast offered sexual favors to those with extra cash; in other halls, prostitutes offered services in the balconies. So popular did these seats become that newer halls were specially designed to accommodate this particular clientele. The Bird Cage did not have a green room or a tier of seats but it did have its boxes. And their reputation quickly grew.

To some families it was as if Sodom and Gomorrah had again risen in the desert. One woman remembered her family passing through Tombstone when she was about sixteen years old. So intimidated was the family by the reputation of Allen Street and the rumors of lawlessness and debauchery that they stayed the night with doors locked and fears dominant. "It was a wild place," she said. "We shrank from any more contact with its inhabitants than was absolutely necessary." The mother of the family was so terrified of the place that the group left town the next morning without eating breakfast.

As was the case with many other frontier towns, prostitution in Tombstone was not illegal; it was taxed. Civic leaders made only perfunctory efforts even to segregate it from the rest of the community. Indeed, in March 1882, the Tombstone city council voted to remove existing restrictions on the location of brothels, despite the objections of a few of the residents of the "respectable" community. For every person or persons engaged in keeping a house of ill fame where wines and spirituous liquors were dispensed—places like the Bird Cage Theatre—the price was twenty dollars a month. For many years, the revenue collected from the sale of these licenses was the sole source of financial support for the schools of the town. The prostitutes were also required to pay a fee. A woman who called herself The Gold Dollar, for example, paid her seven dollars for a city license, as did Mollie Williams.

Tombstone had a symbiotic relationship with the flourishing vice industry. It was supported by most of the overwhelmingly male population of the town. Many of the lawmen and city councilmen themselves used the services of prostitutes. Vice helped pay the city's bills.

At times, the breezes of moral reform wafted through town, prompting arrests even for the crime of using indelicate language. If Tombstone had sustained such an arrest policy against those who used indelicate language for any length of time, the court system would have choked to death. Such outrage was irregular and mostly feigned.

"A fallen angel was arrested last Wednesday," a newspaper related, "on a charge of using profane and indecent language and had a hearing before

Justice Hawke in the afternoon. The said angel vehemently denied the charge in terms so strong that His Honor turned pale and nearly fainted. Restoratives were applied and the court was able to gasp 'twenty dollars!' The necessary coin was put up and His Honor is thinking seriously of taking a week off and fumigating the courtroom."

For Tombstone, prostitution was an integral segment of a society dominated by lonely men. Tombstone resident Ed Wittig later remembered that the town had more than a hundred "Painted Ladies." They were no trouble to the police, he said; they were "of mixed races and had to be examined by a Physician every two weeks to determine whether they were diseased or not. They were good spenders, and dressed in the heights of fashion and always contributed to any public subscription to be raised for charity or church work in the vicinity."

There were periods of crisis in Tombstone—times of fire, and disease, and other dangers—when many of the distinctions blurred into common humanity. It was at those times that some of the parlor houses acted as temporary hospitals, and the prostitutes from the Bird Cage and other houses acted as nurses. Many successful community efforts were accomplished with money donated by vice barons and mistresses of Tombstone. "The women of the camp's 'nether world' were the first to respond," remembered one Tombstone resident, "and sometimes came near to bearing the whole load."

Some proprietors of bordellos managed to advertise their wares. Madame Moustache, madam of an establishment of French girls, would often rent a carriage and take the women, sporting their fanciest outfits and feathers, for a ride around town to smile and wave to the citizenry.

At Blonde Marie's, the ambience and taste inclined to the more refined, with the hostesses reputedly imported from the higher-class French syndicate. If most of the girls could speak only a smidgen of French, and that with a labored accent, most of the customers did not know the difference.

There seemed to be someone available for almost anyone. One establishment passed out cards with the following advertisement: "Elderly gentlemen would do well to ask for Maxine in the upper parlor. She is especially adept at coping with matters peculiar to advanced age and a general run-down condition."

A slowly growing population of women had nothing to do with the brothels and dance halls. They were the wives of professional men who established businesses in the town; a few were the wives of miners. Some were professionals themselves, like Addie Bourland, dressmaker, and Nellie Cashman, restaurant owner and miner. There were schoolteachers, those who ran boardinghouses or opened retail stores, and there was even a woman blacksmith in the area of Tombstone.

Some businesswomen of Tombstone worked closely with the prostitutes. Many of the more prosperous prostitutes could afford the radiant attire imported from San Francisco and the East Coast. Others less well-off made their own clothes or relied on the skills of local entrepreneurs such as Helen Yonge Lind. During Tombstone's riotous times, Helen Lind and her husband, John, both artists, ran a drugstore on Allen Street. To supplement the family income, she converted part of their home into a dressmaking establishment. It was there that she fashioned many of the chic gowns for the women John called "bawdy ladies."

But the shady ladies of Tombstone and the other population of women stayed mostly apart. One Tombstone resident wrote, "To be sure, there are frequent dances, which I have heard called 'respectable,' but as long as so many members of the *demi-monder*, who are very numerous and very showy here, patronize them, many honest women will hesitate to attend."

Many of the prostitutes and dance-hall girls did attend church services on Sundays, but the classes rarely mingled. Indeed, an unwritten commandment among the so-called respectable class of women in town dictated that they not even walk on the Bird Cage side of Allen Street. Preferring, at least in public, to ignore prostitution altogether, "respectable" women often referred to the women in this profession simply as "single women" and their men visitors as "gentlemen callers."

But the class and society hatreds took their toll. One girl from the Bird

Cage said later, "Them women always looked down their noses at us—excepting when they needed some money for a charity. Then—they'd come down and ask us girls."

A Rung Below

Thousands of young women who flocked to the West searching for freedom and wealth, many ill-prepared for what lay in store, found wretchedness, not fortune. Many of the regular hostesses of the Bird Cage lived alongside other young prostitutes of lesser social standing in a section of housing near the theater, made up of cheap shacks. Although many of the women attempted to make their own private rooms as clean and personal as possible, they endured a spartan living. For most, it was a dignity-shattering existence.

Many of the houses of prostitution were located east of the Bird Cage. At Rowdy Kate Lowe's, the girls and the atmosphere were more like the Dodge City roughhouses that she had left behind a few years earlier.

For all the women, the life was challenging. A miner wrote later: "The mortality amongst these girls was awful, especially those who lived in those cheap, draughty pneumonia inducing shacks immediately surrounding the Bird Cage saloon. Drinking so much booze combined with pneumonia and the hard life they led caused them to go by the scores."

Although the dancers and hostesses of the Bird Cage were several steps up the ladder from most of the prostitutes of Tombstone, the ladder itself was always precarious. Carmelita Gimenes, a well-known Bird Cage singer, was living with Frederick Baker, a young actor who had also taken a job at the Bird Cage. Baker recalled, "All I know, I have been living with her for four or five months. A few nights ago after we got through work at the Bird Cage Theatre where we are both employed . . . she commenced crying. . . . I have noticed of late that she was not in her right spirits, rather downhearted and melancholy." Carmelita ended her career and her life with a dose of rat poison.

For the girls of the Bird Cage, the irony of their lives could not have been more sharp. Inside the Bird Cage, they strutted and preened, tantalized and teased, flexing a degree of power and control. Most of them liked to think that the theater or entertainment aspect of their job was their real profession. But for many, it was not. And outside, they were mostly lonely and alone, broke and sick. But at least the women of the Bird Cage kept out of Pascual Negro's and other dives of that ilk or the cribs on Sixth Street.

Indeed, some moved on to greater elegance. Samantha Taylor, a dancer at the Bird Cage, later married and ran the San Jose House, one of the many business enterprises owned by Ed Schieffelin. One Tombstone resident euphemistically called the San Jose House "the sportingest boarding-house in Tombstone," a place where the well-heeled could meet the classiest women of loose commerce. Wyatt Earp, who visited the San Jose House on a number of occasions, later remembered Samantha as "Mrs. Fallon." Wyatt had good reason to visit the place—it was near his favorite ice cream store and, for a time, a certain close acquaintance, Josephine Sarah Marcus, resided there.

Little Gertie, The Gold Dollar, was a diminutive, golden-haired prostitute who carried on most of her business on Sixth Street and was named after a one-dollar coin being minted in the United States that was smaller than a dime. Living with a tinhorn gambler named Billy Milgreen, Gertie made it clear that no other denizens of the red-light district would ever get their hands on him. None ever did until the arrival of Margarita. Sultry and dark, the prostitute from Mexico moved in on Billy. The Gold Dollar warned her rival; she warned her lover. Billy pledged fidelity; Margarita pledged nothing.

During a card game one evening in the Bird Cage, Margarita strutted around the table, teasing Billy, flaunting her considerable charms, even sitting on his lap. From another position in the Bird Cage, Gertie watched Margarita's advances. Enraged, she suddenly charged across the room, grabbed Margarita by her long, black hair. Margarita fought with long, sharp nails; Gertie fought with a long knife she pulled from her garter belt.

It was quickly over, the knife lodging in the Mexican girl's side. In the Boot Hill cemetery, a tombstone reads: "Margarita Stabbed by Gold Dollar." Because of the extenuating circumstances, Tombstone authorities did not prosecute the well-known prostitute. She soon left Tombstone.

Like the drifting gunmen on the frontier and the hobo populations that would emerge in the United States with the growth of the railroads, prostitutes in the frontier West used monikers both to conceal their real identities and to establish new ones. For whatever individual personal and psychological reasons, they, like the gunslingers and hoboes, had left their pasts and their surnames behind. They took names that reflected personal or physical characteristics, birthplaces, or talents. They were now Irish Mag, Faro Nell, and Dutch Annie.

In the new mining towns like Tombstone and in establishments like the Bird Cage, they could attempt to start over. Their backgrounds were as different as the women themselves. Some were from broken homes; others from established families. Some were driven by wanderlust; others had been scrapped early in their lives by lovers, husbands, or families. Many were hooked on booze and drugs.

In Tombstone some of the prostitutes became near mythic figures—Big Nose Kate, who carried on a long, tempestuous relationship with Doc Holliday; Madame Blonde Marie; and Eleanora Dumont aka Madame Moustache, for whom Tombstone was only the most recent stop in a legendary life of gambling and whoring. And there was Crazy Horse Lil, large of stature, short of patience, and with billingsgate language to back it all up, who fought men and women alike in the Bird Cage. She was credited with the following economic justification for her profession: "The wages of sin are a damn sight higher," she said, "than the wages of virtue." But sadly for most prostitutes in Tombstone, including those of the Bird Cage, Lil's remark somehow never rang true.

CHAPTER 8

The Mystery of Sadie Earp

The sheer gown, hiding nothing underneath, drapes over her body, its piercing V neckline plunging down to her folded hands in front. Her head is slightly tilted back, eyes half-closed, mouth petulant, almost mocking, ebony-colored hair sweeping back down her shoulders. She was enough to inspire Harlequin prose.

The photograph was taken in 1881 . . . or was it 1914? In the 1993 film *Tombstone,* the photographer Cornelius Fly is in the act of photographing the sensual woman in the famous pose just minutes before the O.K. Corral shootout. But in reality, she was nowhere near Fly's when the fight broke out.

At an auction in New York in 1998, Sotheby's hiked the bid on the hand-tinted picture to $2,875. It was a photo, said Sotheby's, of Josephine Sarah Marcus Earp, one of the wives of Wyatt Earp, and former dancer at the Bird Cage Theatre. But was it?

Josephine Sarah Marcus, who liked to be called Sadie, was the daughter of a Jewish baker and his wife. Born in Brooklyn, New York, in 1861, she was the third of four children of German-Jewish immigrants Sophie and Henry Hyman Marcus. When she was seven years old, the family moved to San Francisco.

In her memoirs, Josephine recalled: "My blood demanded excitement, variety and change. I sensed that fact before I was very old." In 1879 the Pauline Markham Theater Company prepared to take *H.M.S. Pinafore* on the road through the Southwest. The gorgeous young woman, who as a teenager had taken dance lessons in San Francisco, satisfied both her restlessness and her ambition by slipping away with the troupe as part of the cast.

Sadie and Johnny

By the time the acting troupe arrived in Prescott, Arizona, the family had managed to alert friends, who apprehended the wayward teenager and sent her back to San Francisco. Nevertheless, Sadie had already met Johnny Behan, a divorced, bankrupt dandy who had just become sheriff of newly formed Cochise County. The bewitched but duplicitous Johnny wrote to Sadie in California, pledging his love and future marriage. Once again, she left San Francisco, this time expecting to be married.

Sadie and the recently divorced Johnny arrived in Tombstone in 1880. They lived together, along with Johnny's son, Albert, but the two did not marry. According to author Stuart Lake, Wyatt Earp's early biographer, "Bat Masterson, and a score of old-timers, have told me that she was the belle of the honkytonks, the prettiest dame in three hundred or so of her kind. Johnny Behan was a notorious 'chaser' and a free spender making lots of money. He persuaded the

Sheriff John Behan. (Courtesy of the Arizona Department of Library, Archives, and Public Records.)

beautiful Sadie to leave the honkytonk and set her up as his 'girl,' after which she was known in Tombstone as Sadie Behan." A local newspaper said she would be a "lady anywhere."

After living with Behan for a time, Sadie found him cavorting with another woman and, in the summer of 1881, moved out. For a few months she was on her own and some historians and history buffs suggest that she turned briefly to prostitution. The evidence for such assertions is scant but suggestive. For example, Doc Holliday once told Denver reporters that he had quarreled with Johnny Behan and had "told him in the presence of a crowd that he was gambling with money which I had given his woman."

Sadie and Wyatt

Others claim that when the Bird Cage Theatre opened its doors late in 1881, Sadie took a job as a showgirl and perhaps turned to prostitution for a time, under the name of Sadie Jo. But, once again, the evidence that exists is wispy thin and circumstantial. Nevertheless, Sadie soon riveted her attention on the most dashing man in town, Wyatt Earp, then living in an uneasy peace with his common-law wife, Mattie. Around the time of the O.K. Corral shootout in October 1881, Sadie and Wyatt ignited a relationship that would last for the rest of his life. Whatever the truth, the legend was planted and flowers to this day: the romance of the frontier lawman and the lovely dove of the Bird Cage. Some locals will point out a room in the lower floors of the Bird Cage as the exact spot in which Wyatt and his showgirl carried on their dalliances.

A few months after the opening of the Bird Cage, Morgan Earp became the latest casualty of the war between the Cowboys and the Earp faction. Sometime before ten P.M. on a Saturday night in March 1882, Morgan and some friends were at Schieffelin Hall for the opening night of William Horace Lingard and Company's *Stolen Kisses,* a play advertised to give the audience incessant laughter. After the performance, he joined Wyatt and others for some billiards at Campbell and Hatch's saloon, just down Allen Street from the Bird Cage.

As he stood with his back to the glass door in the rear of the room that opens out upon the alley, a bullet blasted through the glass. As the *Epitaph* reported, at the time the shot was fired Morgan was "standing within ten feet of the door, and the assassin standing near enough to see his position, took aim for about the middle of his person, shooting through the upper portion of the whitened glass. The bullet entered the right side of the abdomen, passing through the spinal column, completely shattering it, emerging on the left side, passing the length of the room. . . ."

A second shot, evidently intended for Wyatt, ripped into the wall above his head. Morgan fell instantly upon the first fire and lived only about one hour. Wyatt and others in the room rushed to his side, picked him up, and moved him to another room. The doctors who were called could do nothing. "In a few brief moments he breathed his last," the report said, "surrounded by his brothers, Wyatt, Virgil, James and Warren with the wives of Virgil and James and a few of his most intimate friends. Notwithstanding the intensity of his mortal agony, not a word of complaint escaped his lips, and all that were heard, except those whispered into the ear of his brother and known only to him were, "Don't, I can't stand it. This is the last game of pool I'll ever play."

Morgan Earp's assassination triggered a series of events that would forever separate Wyatt Earp and Sadie from Tombstone. During the months following the shooting, the town of Tombstone did seem something like a war zone, with unprecedented numbers of killings, as the Earps and the Cowboys traded attacks.

For Wyatt, the killing of his brother was an act to be met with total retribution. Gone now were any thoughts of the lawman about law and justice and trials and evidence; this was the time for a vendetta. He and his friends left Tombstone to follow and exterminate Morgan's killers. East along Allen Street and past the Bird Cage and out of town rode Wyatt Earp, Doc Holliday, and four others, past throngs of people standing on the wooden sidewalks.

Portrait of woman some think is Josephine Sarah Marcus Earp. (Courtesy of Roger A. Bruns.)

"Each of the horsemen were armed with a shotgun, Winchester rifle and two revolvers, and at least 100 rounds of ammunition," a reporter noted. "All sorts of rumors were rife upon the streets during the afternoon and evening, but until 6 o'clock no one knew to a certainty which direction, after leaving the city, the horsemen had taken. . . . there seems no reason to doubt them, a bloody combat will surely be the result."

Sadie and the Truth

One of Morgan's killers was blasted into eternity in Tucson's train yard, a few hours' ride away, and others soon followed. After Wyatt and his friends systematically tracked down and wiped out, one by one, all those he believed responsible for Morgan's death, he and Sadie moved on. After the spring of 1882, the man whose name is forever linked in history to Tombstone would never set foot in it again.

Sadie traveled with Wyatt throughout the West, especially San Francisco, at times with her parents. By the 1920s, the two were into mining and oil ventures and the promotion of a movie about Wyatt's exploits. They were also helping journalist Stuart Lake, who had undertaken a major biography of Wyatt. After Earp died in 1929, she and Lake warred about the book's commercialization and his unflattering depiction of her role in Wyatt's life. *Wyatt Earp: Frontier Marshal,* with many passages removed, appeared in 1931. It fueled years of Earpmania. The story she told to Lake, and which she later recorded in her own memoirs, omitted nearly all references to her activities in Tombstone. She did not mention the Bird Cage Theatre.

Was Earp a heroic western lawman fighting for law and order? Or a self-promoting, greedy speculator on the edges of respectability? Or a ruthless murderer? Was she an actress of uncommon beauty wrapped in a quintessential love match with an American hero? Was she a reckless, young runaway, drawn into dubious liaisons? Was she a Bird Cage performer? Or were they both a mixture of these conflicting images and portraits?

Wyatt Earp is now a figure upon whom historians as well as the general public have passed personal judgment. As elusive facts surrounding his life and loves and the shades of doubt and hints of fact are argued and researched, opinions are mostly solidified. His unquestioned fearlessness and magnetic personal bearing are weighed against a life given over mostly to speculation and, at a critical time, to violent retribution—and the judges choose sides. They did in Tombstone over a hundred years ago and they do now. Nevertheless, that the significance of his life, even in the Tombstone years, has been warped beyond recognition cannot be denied.

For Josephine Sarah Marcus Earp, even her name is now a matter of debate. When she was in Tombstone, the showgirl went by the name of Sadie. Later, in California, as she wrote her memoirs and shadowed some of the details of her times in Tombstone, she began to call herself Josie and her friends did too. When Josie looked back on Sadie's days on the frontier, much of the story became obscure.

When she left Johnny Behan in Tombstone in 1881 and lived for a time on her own, she may have worked at the new Bird Cage Theatre. But there is no convincing evidence. The young woman who had left home to travel across dangerous Indian territory in search of excitement was both adventuresome and reckless. When her relationship to her older paramour Behan exploded, she may have turned briefly to prostitution. There were rumors to that effect but again no convincing evidence.

And what of the beguiling photograph? Sotheby's got it wrong. They identified the photograph as Sadie Earp and dated the photo as 1914. It cannot be both. If the photo is actually that of Sadie, it had to have been taken in 1881 when she was still a young woman.

The cameo photo recently sold by Sotheby's, purportedly of young Sadie, has become a bone of historical contention in Earpmania circles. Writer Glenn Boyer, author of several books on Tombstone, a man whose scholarship has been under attack by a number of detractors who claim he mixes historical creations with fact, has long maintained that Johnny Behan took the photo of her in Tombstone near the time of the incident at the

O.K. Corral. Was this photo just another manifestation of the Bird Cage beauty's willingness to show off her charms?

But Boyer's challengers say the photo is of an unidentified woman, taken in 1914 and clearly not of an 1880s vintage. They have discovered evidence that the photo was circulated by the Pastime Novelty Company (later called the ABC Novelty Company) of Brooklyn, New York. Some copies of the photograph bear the name *Kaloma* and carry a date of 1914. Copies of the photo were widely reproduced on naughty Mexican postcards. Was Kaloma the name of the girl in the picture? No evidence exists.

Boyer says he was given the photo in the mid-fifties by a woman who ran a cantina in Yuma and claimed she had known Josephine Earp. Boyer, the ever-vigilant and careful tracker, says he had doubts about the photo until Ernest Cason, husband of the woman who had helped Josephine write her memoirs, gave Boyer another photo, purportedly of Josephine, that looked remarkably similar to the one he had received in the Yuma cantina.

The search for the historical truth became so intense that photography experts were consulted. Robin Gilliam, history curator at the Silver City Museum in Silver City, New Mexico, says Boyer's photo is not what he claims. "Everything about it suggests that it's an early 20th-century print of an entertainer. . . . it's clearly from that era. The vamp style, the dark eye makeup. It's a completely different style than what would have been considered a sexy pinup girl in the early 1880s. Even if Josephine Earp had been a pinup, she would have done it in a completely different way."

Did Sadie play the Bird Cage? Did Wyatt Earp meet her there? Did she conceal her past in later years or did overeager historians fight over her memory and likeness just as Wyatt Earp and Johnny Behan fought over her affections?

And so the arguments persist. On the question of the mysterious photograph of the sensuously draped young woman, Glenn Boyer deserves the final word. "If it isn't Josie," he says, "it ought to be."

CHAPTER 9

Tall Tales and Somewhat True

From the raucous confines of the Bird Cage, many stories traveled far in their journeys from witness accounts to folklore. Some of the stories made their way to the pages of contemporary newspapers; others first gained life in letters and in tales handed down. Later, as authors and other interviewers talked with old-timers years after the events on the frontier, the stories took on new shapes and forms. Sometimes the occurrences could be verified by witnesses, sometimes not.

The Bird Cage and the
Blood Red Streets of Tombstone

Take the case of a dancer named Annie Ashley. Annie once told an interviewer that rival gangs and feudists would often sit on opposite sides of the Bird Cage, taunting and shouting at each other during the performances. Sometimes they would literally gun each other down right there inside the theater. In an almost ritualistic, rehearsed fashion, she remembered, the performers would drop to the floor at the first sign of trouble and lie flat on their stomachs. As soon as the shooting started, the theater lights would suddenly go out, screams would fill the room, and the performers would hit the boards of the stage.

Luridly, feverishly, Annie continued to astonish her interviewer. She described how the fight would quiet down, a kind of deadly quiet meant to deceive the enemy, and then it would all flare up again. The lights would again go out, the performers would once more drop on their stomachs, and the bullets would again fly. Sometimes the violence would get so severe in town, Annie contended, that blood literally flowed along Tombstone's dirt streets. Sixteen men, she said, once "sprawled out in their own blood—dead." All in all, she said, it was a singular experience for a young performer. "Earning money then," she recalled, "was exciting." And Annie survived it all. Annie survived because most of her recollections were fanciful.

Lotta Crabtree Plays the Bird Cage

She was a radiant performer, one of the acclaimed actresses of the day. She was the toast of San Francisco. Whether delivering with lilting voice a tearful ballad or quick-picking a banjo, Lotta Crabtree thrilled audiences in the concert halls, mining camps, variety shows, and amusement parks across the land. By the beginning of the Civil War she was Miss Lotta, the San Francisco Favorite. By 1870, she had her own touring company and was earning a fortune. Unpredictable, impulsive, and devilish, she was five-foot-two and had light red hair, which she sprinkled sparingly with cayenne pepper for her performances. She smoked thin black cigars off stage.

In Tombstone, years after its glory days, some residents talked about the time Lotta played the Bird Cage, about the massive crowd that welcomed her to town, about her entrancing appearance, and about the many miners, cowboys, and soldiers who, that day, fell in love. Ed Wittig Jr., son of the

Bird Cage orchestra leader, claimed he saw Lotta there.

It apparently never happened. It is true that Lotta's brother, Jack Crabtree, visited Tombstone many times and also true that Jack told folks in Tombstone that he planned to build a theater and intended to invite his sister to appear at its opening. But there is no evidence that he ever built the theater or that Lotta ever came to town. Tombstone had its own legends. But it almost certainly did not have Lotta Crabtree on the stage at the Bird Cage.

Warblings of the Tombstone Nightingale

Another tale handed down: During one evening's entertainment, a dapper gunslinger was being pleased in his box by a bevy of beauties. On stage a singer who called herself the Tombstone Nightingale, the Queen of Song, performed for the audience. Suddenly from the gunslinger's box came a rude shout: "Rotten. Who ever told you you could sing?" The Tombstone Nightingale, used to rowdy behavior, tried to continue but another powerful bellow erupted from the box: "Awful. Rats. Take her out."

This was too much for the proprietor and too much for the crowd. Screams of "Throw him out" reverberated through the Bird Cage. Proprietor Billy Hutchinson responded, ordering the gunslinger tossed out. Billy's bouncers eagerly marched upstairs and, after much scuffling, a body hurtled out of the box across the theater, arms and legs flying, and plopped onto the heads of several horrified spectators below. Silence. Then a great roar of laughter. The body was a suit of clothes stuffed with straw.

The whole thing had been a ruse, a little additional spice for the evening from Billy Hutchinson. But in numerous accounts of this incident at the Bird Cage, the gunslinger is actually identified as Russian Bill Tettenborn, who, the legend goes, occupied a Bird Cage box right next to the stage night after night. The exotic Bill, who claimed lineage to Russian nobility, was actually a fledgling rustler whose father was reportedly a Russian of less than noble station. As with many legends born within the confines of the Bird Cage, this one has a problem. Russian Bill had been ingloriously hanged in a New Mexico town a month before the Bird Cage Theatre opened. The name of the town, incidentally, was Shakespeare.

Clothesless in Tombstone

Charles L. Cummings, one-time owner of the Bird Cage, liked to tell the story of the visiting stock company that was stranded in Tombstone because the sheriff confiscated the performers' trunks for failure to pay their board bill. The sheriff accomplished his civic duty at the same time that many of the women entertainers were in action at the Bird Cage, dressed in their stage outfits. When they returned to their rooms after the performance, their clothes were gone.

"Those girls had to go about the city for days with nothing but their tights to cover them," Cummings told a *Star* reporter in 1929. "Probably some shocked individuals got their clothing released, for eventually the troupe left the city."

Cummings's story may have been the embellished incarnation of the experience of the English Opera Company when it visited Tombstone in 1879. That company's baggage was confiscated by the sheriff temporarily on the complaint of Mr. A. E. Fay of the *Nugget,* who claimed that the company had underpaid its bill.

But even if dates, individuals, and details about the Bird Cage troupe remain hidden, whether the story is apocryphal or true, it sustained its humor, if not its credibility, for decades.

The Handkerchief Duel

Doc Holliday was often seen playing faro at the Bird Cage. On one occasion, the story goes, a few months after the altercation west of Cornelius

Cornet player at the Bird Cage. (Courtesy of the Tombstone Courthouse State Historic Park.)

Fly's house, the intemperate gunslinger Johnny Ringo, ally of the Clantons, confronted the equally intemperate dentist/cardplayer and friend of the Earps, an individual for whom Ringo had the utmost contempt. When Johnny passed Holliday's table, Doc, in his usual alcohol-induced stupor, remarked, "Care to buck the tiger, Johnny? It's the gutsiest game in town."

Offended by this seemingly innocuous remark, Ringo spun around, whipped off his bandanna, and challenged Holliday: "Care to grab the other end of this bandanna? It's the deadliest game in town."

Never one to back off, Doc rose, smiled, looked Ringo in the eye and responded, "Sure, Johnny, I'm your huckleberry and this may be my lucky day." Many men who played the bandanna game—grabbing opposite ends of the cloth, drawing pistols, and firing at point-blank range—often ended up with a draw: both of them dead. Only the intervention at the last second of another Bird Cage cardplayer who pulled Ringo away as the two fired, it is said, saved them from probable extinction. The event has gone down in Bird Cage lore as The Handkerchief Duel.

John Ringo came to Arizona after a scrape with the law in Texas. He was well educated, some old-timers claimed, and one of his favorite books was said to be *Ben Hur*. Ringo threw in with former cellmate and legendary shootist William "Curly Bill" Brocious. Tombstone folks swore that Ringo could place a liquor bottle on its side on a fence post twenty-five feet away and fire a .44 slug down the neck of the bottle, blowing out the bottom.

In 1872 a young man from Georgia named John Holliday earned a degree of Doctor of Dental Surgery at the Pennsylvania College of Dental Surgery and soon entered practice in Atlanta. Holliday's life and career were soon ravaged; he was diagnosed with tuberculosis. The consensus of various doctors was that he had only a few months to live, but they suggested that a move to a drier climate might prolong his life. Doc headed west and took up gambling, something for which he had a natural affinity. He also had an affinity for knives and guns. In Texas and Dodge City, he began to earn a name as a sharpster, deadly and unpredictable, a man with little to lose. He struck up a friendship with Wyatt Earp in Dodge City, met up with him again in Tombstone, and was at his side at the great shootout.

Ringo and Doc Holliday had no use for each other. But is the story of the confrontation another elaborate legend ensnared by the rolling tumbleweed of Bird Cage mystique? It is clear from the evidence that Doc and Ringo did confront each other in mid-January 1882. It is also clear, however, that those who reported on the altercation said that it occurred on the street, not in the Bird Cage.

George Parsons, who left a daily journal, noted that he saw the whole thing go down as he was walking down the street: "Ringo and Doc Holliday came nearly having it with pistols. . . . One with hand in breast pocket and the other probably ready. Earps just beyond. Crowded street and looked like another battle. Police vigilant for once, and both disarmed."

Other reports also place the action in the street. The *Tucson Weekly Citizen* gave the exact location: "A difficulty occurred yesterday afternoon in front of the Occidental Saloon, Allen Street, between John Ringo and Doc Holliday, that very nearly terminated in bloodshed. The parties had been on bad terms for some time past, and meeting yesterday morning words were exchanged and both parties stepped back, placing their hands on their weapons with the intention of drawing and using them. Fortunately chief of police Flynn was at hand and placed both parties under arrest."

Nothing about a game of faro, nothing about the Bird Cage Theatre. That tumbleweed had struck again.

Bringing Redemption to the Bird Cage

Although some of the tales collided with countervailing facts, the tales, nevertheless, survived in one form or another. And in all of this history and lore, some stories survive with a degree of integrity not achieved by others. For example:

A Methodist preacher named Jospeh McCann once insisted on climbing onto the Bird Cage stage one Sunday morning to bellow out a sermon, an action he probably believed akin to Daniel challenging the lions in their den. Like most itinerant preachers roaming the Southwest, McCann looked very much like a gambler, with his long black coat, white shirt, and string tie, and he did find his audience attentive to a point. Some of them, groggy from several hours of drink and merriment, puzzled over this unique Bird Cage offering. With much flourish, McCann uttered such memorable lines as:

I'll tell you who the Lord loves best,
It's the shouting Methodist!

Charles Andress brought his "Carnival of Novelties and Trained Animal Show" to the Bird Cage. (Courtesy of the Arizona State Historical Society.)

When he finished, they asked for more. They yelled for him to dance. Shocked, McCann refused. "Indeed not," he thundered, "I am a minister of the Gospel!" After a second request produced the same response, one of the rowdies drew a pistol and shot off the reverend's boot heel. The instinct of self-preservation finally triggered, he danced, not very well according to reports. Soon he was on a stage headed east.

The story of the dancing minister has been told and retold in accounts of Tombstone's finest hours. The incident did occur. The question is where it occurred or if it occurred more than once. According to the diarist George Parsons, the professional troublemaker Curly Bill Brosius broke into a religious service in Charleston, Arizona, announced to the congregation that he was going to test the religiosity of the preacher, and began to spray bullets around his feet, prompting the preacher to dance a jig. Parsons identified the minister as McKane, "the one Curly Bill made dance and commanded to preach and pray, shot out lights, etc., at Charleston recently." The incident, also reported by the *San Francisco Daily Report,* took place in May 1881, half a year before the Bird Cage Theatre opened.

It is possible that preacher McCann was humiliated in such a fashion more than one time. If so, it is not surprising that he took that stage out of Arizona for good.

Bullets

Among the more imaginative performances at the Bird Cage was a bullet-catching act where a magician would have an assistant shoot blanks at him. He would then spit bullets out of his mouth as if he had caught them in his teeth, an extraordinarily inane act even for an audience like the one in the Bird Cage. Sure enough, one drunken cowboy tried to help with the act by shooting more bullets to be caught by the magician. Luckily a friend deflected his hand. Years later, folks in the Bird Cage still called attention to the specific bullet holes that fortunately hit the stage and not the magic man.

More gunplay entertainment: A Bird Cage beauty was standing on the stage waiting for a sharpshooter to knock an apple off her head. Off to the side of the stage stood Pat Holland, the town's newly elected coroner and a noted marksman himself. As the shooter carefully and methodically squinted down the barrel, the tension mounting, the coroner for some reason became increasingly impatient with the agonizingly slow pace of things on the stage. Suddenly he grabbed an old stage prop musket, assuming it was loaded only with powder and a paper wad, took aim at the apple and fired. The musket was not loaded with powder and a paper wad; it was loaded with real buckshot. One of the cast had taken it rabbit hunting that afternoon and had not returned the weapon to its innocent stage condition.

It was fortunate that Pat Holland was a good shot. The *Territorial Enterprise* of Virginia City reported that the buckshot that roared across the Bird Cage stage ripped the apple off the girl's head, blasting it to mush. Also, "a bunch of hair, half as big as a man's fist, was carried across the stage and struck the opposite wall."

Another good story from the Bird Cage. Its truth in all of the particulars: hazy at best.

Run Eliza!

On one memorable occasion, the Bird Cage offered a production of *Uncle Tom's Cabin*. Already a classic only two decades after the Civil War, Harriet Beecher Stowe's play was so popular across the United States that many actors and companies, called Tommers and Tom Shows, traveled the country performing it.

The productions were as varied as the troupes, drawing from minstrel acts, circus attractions, and trained animal shows. One particular Tom Show in 1879 bore such faint resemblance to Stowe's masterpiece that one critic suggested the production be titled *The Cake Walk, with Spasmodic Glimpses of Uncle Tom and His Newly Painted Cabin*.

It was American literature as spectacle, as advertisements proclaimed: "Eliza's Escape on the Floating Ice Followed at Full Speed by the Furious Pack of Panting Bloodhounds Goaded on to Madness by their less Savage Master—THE MOST THRILLING SCENE EVER DEPICTED."

Several promoters in the 1870s decided that Eliza's flight to freedom from Kentucky over the frozen Ohio River would be enlivened by the participation of actual snarling dogs. The bloodhounds or mastiffs were such great hits that they became a staple for most productions.

The troupe playing the Bird Cage featured one such large animal. Charles "Uncle Charley" Andress, old-time showman and magician and creator of Andress's Carnival of Novelties and Trained Animal Show, an extravaganza that offered "Performing Fleas" as well as "The Learned Pig," also appeared that night at the Bird Cage. Years later, when he looked back over his long, eccentric career, Charley remembered this night as one of the most bizarre.

As Eliza fled the slave catchers and their bloodhound over the simulated ice floes, one member of the audience found the performance much too riveting. The well-meaning, concerned, but liquor-sotted cowboy, emotionally caught up in the action, decided to save Eliza from the fangs of the slavering pursuer. He shot it.

"After something of a fight," the *Star* reported, "the cowboy was lodged in jail and the show continued minus one good hound. . . . The cowboy was somewhat the worse for his beating when he sobered up, but was penitent and shed tears over the dead dog, offering money and his pony in recompense."

And the stories roll on . . .

CHAPTER 10

Wrestlin' and Hoofin', Dancin' and Singin'

On November 13, 1882, the Bird Cage featured the artistic clog dancing and "Ethiopian acting" and blackface comedy of Joe Bignon. One of the newspaper reporters who witnessed Bignon on stage said it was amazing the performer didn't break his neck in some of his reckless jumps. A rising western variety-stage performer and promoter, Bignon was the proprietor and manager of the Park Theatre in Tucson. The delights of Allen Street often lured him to Tombstone. Unlike Tucson, the new Silverado to the south seemed to be the San Francisco of the prairie, Bignon thought. Allen Street could be the next Barbary Coast and Joe wanted to be at the center of it all. He would be back.

Bird Cage patrons saw a smorgasbord of entertainers. They saw leg shows, bawdy skits, and boisterous variety acts. They saw the Healy Brothers, who, according to a handbill, offered "grotesque Dancing, Leg Mania and Contortion Feats. . . ." They saw the athletic jig dancer Pearl

Ardine. And there was Mollie Archer, who, according to the *Daily Nugget*, ranked "foremost as character singer and impersonator of male characters." Some of the entertainers were big time.

A handbill of the day didn't spare the superlatives:

BIRD CAGE THEATER
WM. HUTCHINSON . . . PROP'R
THE POPULAR RESORT OF TOMBSTONE
GREATEST SUCCESS OF THE DAY–
HOUSES CROWDED NIGHTLY

Will Shortly Appear
JERRY HART
Greatest Negro Comedian and End Man.

MISS LEO HART
Who will appear in a new and unique album of
popular songs

Great Success of
MISS CORA VANE
Who acknowledges no superior as a serio-comic vocalist

ALSO
Our unrivaled stock company consisting of
M'lle De Granville, Lottie Hutchinson
Billy Clayton, Irene Baker
And
MULLIGAN AND SHEEHAN
The Great Irish Comedians

ADMISSION 50 CENTS. PRIVATE BOXES $2.50

The Education of a Vaudevillian

Comedian Eddie Foy had played some of the roughest variety theaters in the West, including the riotous Bella Union in San Francisco. For a time he appeared in the starring role in *Little Robinson Crusoe,* produced by the American Burlesque Company.

In Dodge City in 1878, the cocky young Foy appeared on the stage of the Comique, a combination saloon, dance hall, gambling house, and theater, much like the Bird Cage. Although the swaggering youngster routinely poked fun at the rough drifters and ranch hands, he went too far on one occasion. Some of the audience roped the young man off the stage, dunked him in a horse trough, and rode him around on horseback. When he took the hazing in stride—"I was determined to be nonchalant," he said—the locals finally accepted the comedian as a brother. One Dodge City merchant said later of Foy: "Nothing he could say or do offended them. They made a little god of him."

On another occasion in Dodge, while calling a square dance, Eddie found himself in the middle of a shootout. When bullets starting flying from the street through the saloon walls as well as through the windows, "Bat Masterson was just in the act of dealing a game of Spanish Monte with Doc Holliday," Eddie remembered, "and I was impressed by the instantaneous manner in which they flattened out like pancakes on the floor." Eddie did suffer a casualty on that occasion. He had just purchased an eleven-dollar suit and had left the coat hanging in the dressing room. When he returned after the carnage, the garment, still smoldering, had been pierced in three places.

Thus when the comedian visited Tombstone and the Bird Cage, he was no stranger to western variety theaters: "Our engagement was at a concert hall known as the Bird Cage Varieties. . . . We seemed to make good and could have stayed longer. Incidentally, let me say that I was never shot at nor made the target for eggs or cabbage by dissatisfied patrons in those

Eddie Foy at the Bird Cage. (Courtesy of the Arizona State Historical Society.)

mining camp honkytonks, nor did I ever see any other actor suffer such indignity. It is true that the audience sometimes expressed its approval or disapproval rather emphatically; but I never saw any violence offered save by some fellow who was drunk and irresponsible."

Foy later looked back on his work on the early western stages with much fondness and nostalgia. In the crowds of gamblers, gunfighters, miners, and desperadoes, he had found genuine friendship and respect. The stage, he said, was for those men a special infatuation, an escape that was essential for their lives—laughter after the grueling days, relief from the sun and the sweat, escape in the form of a devilish, outrageous comedian who, despite all outward appearances to the contrary, seemed to belong here in the desert.

Eddie Foy later became one of the country's hottest vaudeville acts. The Bird Cage and other western venues had seasoned him well for his later career, a few years and many, many miles down the road.

For the Love of Nola

When the charming comedienne and "premiere danseuse" Nola Forest bounced around the Bird Cage stage bedecked in garlands of flowers, fans, jewelry, and the best finery ever seen in the western desert, it was almost too much for one of Tombstone's most respected residents, a quiet book-keeper named J. P. Wells. So infatuated did the gentleman become with Nola Forest that every night he managed to secure a front-row seat to take in her considerable charms. He was Nola's biggest fan.

Fans sometimes lose control. J. P. Wells, the last person most Tombstone residents would have suspected of criminal activity, decided to put his book-keeping experience to good use. He embezzled eight hundred dollars from his employer, the Boston Mill Company. The *Tombstone Republican* reported that J. P. "lavished money on her in profusion. A number of handsome diamond ornaments worn by her are said to have been the gifts of Wells."

Nola had earned her billboard sobriquet as The People's Choice. There were many besides Wells who admired her. When she completed her engagement at the Bird Cage, she did not leave town with poor J. P. but with another man from whom she had been temporarily estranged— her husband.

After his experience with Nola, Wells's luck never got any better. He reportedly took up with another woman who, according to Tombstone insiders, completed the financial ruin begun by Nola Forest. In June 1886, Wells was reported drowned in the Gila River.

The Manly Arts

Especially on the frontier, manliness was a cult. Prospectors took on the odds and each other. Gunslingers and gamblers did the same. Men battled over women, insults, reputations, and money. And even on the variety stage, machismo reigned.

In February 1884, Tombstone resident George Parsons wrote in his diary: "Wrestling match to a fine house. Milton M. and I on stage. Ed Willson's second, Gates, the San Pedro Wrestler, selected me to keep time but Maurice had a stop watch and I deferred to him. Exciting, two throws in an hour to be made by Willson—one throw in 21 minutes . . . Couldn't get another."

A Greco-Roman wrestler named Peter Schumacher was perhaps the biggest manly-arts attraction of the Bird Cage, even more intimidating than Mlle. Granville, the weight lifter, who was, of course, a woman. Like Granville, Schumacher was also a heavy lifter. An *Epitaph* reporter observed one of the large man's feats: "A ponderous bar of iron, weighing fully 150 pounds, was raised aloft in Mr. Schumacher's hands, and in addition to this was the entire weight of three average sized men, who held on to the projecting ends, and the whole carried about the stage with apparent ease by the Young Hercules." Although most Bird Cage fans understood that not even the legendary Hercules could haul three men and a huge iron bar around a stage, the illusion sufficed.

The Bird Cage organized tournaments featuring Cornish wrestlers, Greco-Roman wrestlers, and weight lifters. It even managed to hold a walking contest at the same time other stage activities were under way. "The money is up, in the hands of one of our responsible citizens and the parties mean business," the Bird Cage advertised. "A track will be in the theatre so as not to discommode the audience, and the match will take place during the performance, commencing at 8 P.M. sharp."

The two competitors, John Forseck and John McGarvin, began walking briskly around a makeshift track constructed inside the Bird Cage and continued an admirable pace. Turn after turn around the inside of the smoky, slippery confines the two men strode—for over six hours. Although the Bird Cage audience was thus treated to the sensual overload of seeing two acts at the same time, the walking contests never caught on as a regular attraction, much to management's chagrin. Somehow, walking seemed woefully inadequate when compared to other of the manly arts.

The Boston Strong Boy Stops in Tombstone

In the spring of 1884, the Bird Cage was visited by the symbol of the manly arts in America, the greatest sports figure of the nineteenth century—although the sport in which he excelled was mostly illegal.

Americans in the late nineteenth century had ready and legal access to many vices, including prostitution and drugs and even cockfighting. They didn't have ready and legal access to one of the most traditional of the manly arts—boxing. The art of self-defense was deemed too barbaric in many states, a spectacle fit only for semisecret locations, often near state lines where combatants and spectators alike could scramble away from law enforcement.

Nevertheless the vicious, bare-knuckle sport had become so popular by the 1880s that when Englishman Joe Goss was pounded into submission by Irishman Paddy Ryan in the eighty-seventh round of a bout at Collier

Station, West Virginia, Ryan became generally recognized as the world champion.

In February 1882, Paddy's reign was over. His conqueror: John L. Sullivan, the Boston Strong Boy. "I am willing to fight any man in the country," John L. declared, anyone, anytime, anywhere, with bare fists, skintight gloves or the padded kind, under any rules. It was manly stuff that John L. peddled, pompous but ingratiating to the masses. But if boxing were a science, as some aficionados claimed, John L. was no scientist. The broad-shouldered former masonry helper simply had a thunderous punch.

In May 1881, on a moonlit barge on the Hudson River just outside the jurisdiction of New York City police, Sullivan traded blows with John Flood, the Bullshead Terror. With the usual crowd of sporting men, hoodlums, workers, dandies, and gamblers roaring their sentiments, the Terror was subdued by the dominant Strong Boy, who knocked or threw him down eight times in fifteen minutes.

John L.'s thrashing of Flood led to a match with champion Ryan near New Orleans on February 5, 1882. The only thing Ryan won that day was the toss of the coin to choose the ring corner. He made John L. face the sun. The champion then offered Sullivan a side bet of one thousand dollars, a wager Sullivan eagerly accepted. In nine rounds, Paddy lost the fight, the money, and nearly his senses. He "hit me like he held a telegraph pole," mumbled the groggy Paddy, shortly after his seconds threw in the sponge.

Sullivan took his championship and his growing public acclaim on the road, offering a thousand dollars to anyone who could stay four rounds with him, Queensberry rules. In theaters, dance halls, and armories across America's heartland and into the West, he took on all comers, from blacksmiths to bullies. Few opponents lasted more than one round. A U.S. district attorney who saw one fight said, "I believe no man living or that has lived for 500 years, of whom we have a record, could stand before Sullivan four rounds."

In spring of 1884, Sullivan took his entourage to Arizona. On March 21, he treated fans to a short but convincing drubbing of two fighters on the

Steve Carroll at the Bird Cage. (Courtesy of the Arizona State Historical Society.)

stage of Tucson's Park Theatre. A few days later he was in Tombstone. It was unfortunate that Allie Sullivan Earp, the wife of Virgil Earp, who had left Tombstone after the infamous fracas between the Earps and Clantons, was not there to greet the boxer. Ever since the Strong Boy's fame had reached the national media, Allie had reminded friends that she was one of Sullivan's relatives.

For a man of John L.'s high-living tastes, a visit to the Bird Cage Theatre was a necessity. James Wolf, a young railroad worker who had traveled to the Southwest to take a job with the Santa Fe Railroad, later remembered seeing the great man at the Bird Cage:

> I never saw him on the stage. He simply stood inside the door, but his mere presence packed the house, and the proprietor put on many extra bartenders. We had a local fly weight champion of about a hundred and fifteen pounds who caused the only disturbance created by Sullivan's visit. While the Champ talked to one of the committee, this mosquito suddenly squared off, tapped John L. on the chin, then stepped away but quickly followed with several more punches and side steps, meanwhile daring the big boy to battle.

Sullivan, whose arms were so large, one man said, that he could probably deck a horse, looked around the Bird Cage, looked down at the flyweight, and grinned. Several Bird Cage patrons pulled off the challenger, reported Mr. Wolf, thus saving his life.

The Bird Cage girls put on their best show for the Strong Boy. "Of course the hostesses of the Bird Cage did their damn best, or worst, to attract his attention," James Wolf remembered. "Different ones of them tried to display her speed or naughtiness by high kicking at the chandeliers or wall bracket lamps, but the big boy would merely turn to the bar and call for a drink. Either he was not a ladies man or he disapproved of their profession." In this speculation, Mr. Wolf was, of course, wrong on both counts. Sullivan had merely decided not to mix his vices that particular evening in the Bird Cage.

John L. stayed several days in the Tombstone area, going underground with the miners. He constantly shook hands everywhere he went and, years later, miners would point to a hand and proudly proclaim that it had shook the hand of the great one. Druggist John Yonge was struck by the friendliness of the famed pugilist and took his children to see him at the house of a friend. At one point during the visit, little Duke Yonge scampered upon the great man's lap.

A small number who shook his hand on the trip did not live long enough to reminisce. Sullivan's visit occurred shortly after a group of bandits robbed a payroll shipment of a copper mining company in Bisbee, killing four people. The convicted killers were in the Tombstone jail awaiting the gallows. Curious, Sullivan asked to see them. They joked and kidded and one of the convicted men, Tex Howard, said to Sullivan, "You are not as big a man as I had imagined, Sullivan. They tell me, though, you can knock any one in the world out in four rounds; is that so?" Sullivan reckoned that it was, indeed, so. Tex then joked that the jailer, a smallish man named Ward, could beat the Great One. "He don't look like a fighter," John L. said. "Well, he ain't," Tex quipped, "but he'll knock five of us out in one round next Friday morning." And so he did.

In the coming years, despite the rigorous barhopping, womanizing, and cross-country celebrity marathon, the Strong Boy continued to reign. In July 1889, three thousand fans crowded an outdoor ring in Richburg, Mississippi, to watch John L. pulverize Jake Kilrain in the blazing sun in what was to be the last championship bare-knuckle fight.

Before a sweltering mob of factory workers and society snobs, gamblers, pickpockets, and grafters of every stripe, Sullivan and Kilrain entered the ring, clad in sheepskin breeches, stockings, leather boots, and plastered with beeswax over their groins for protection against low blows. The excruciating contest went on for seventy-five rounds and lasted two hours and sixteen minutes before Kilrain's boys threw in the towel or, more accurately, a blood-drenched sponge. Sullivan would remain the king for more than three more years. But bare-knuckle fighting, something akin to cockfighting by humans, would be outlawed by most states.

John L. Sullivan's stop at the Bird Cage was not without a touch of irony. Many years later, long after the iron man had surrendered his crown, a vaudeville performer named Erma Gilson remembered seeing the aged fighter performing in a variety hall near Chicago: "We had old John L. Sullivan once, and his stunt was to do some shadow-boxing during the oleo. We girls were forced to wear not only the woolen tights, but a pair of silk tights over them. A moral wave must have struck that town about the time we did."

John L. must have longed for the days of the Bird Cage. No such moral waves had ever plagued Tombstone in its riotous days.

CHAPTER 11

Gambling Mania

Going to the West in the first place was a gamble; everybody on the frontier was by definition a gambler. And wherever the picks broke through to the silver or the gold, gamblers swarmed vulture-like. From Mississippi riverboats, from San Francisco and other California sites, from frontier towns in cattle country, the professional gamblers moved in. Tombstone, as did other boomtowns, welcomed them. Especially for hard-rock mining communities, gambling was a way of life; it took experienced gambling men to run the establishments. Many professional gamblers were men of substance, active in civic matters, contributing both money and effort to schools, churches, and town improvements.

A reporter for the *Star* wrote in March 1881, "The profession of gamblers is as honorable as the members of any stock-exchange in the world—and braver. Their word is as good as their bond." Another wrote, "The fact is, almost every branch of business where large transactions are carried on, partakes largely of the game of chance. The handling of iron, wheat, oil, and coal, in modern times, is much like the shuffling of cards by a faro dealer. If there is more honor or squared dealing in one than the other, the faro dealer has the advantage."

Men such as Wyatt Earp, for example, looked back at their careers at the gambling tables with as much pride or disappointment as they did at other aspects of their lives, such as investing in silver mines. Years after the events, they could remember a card hand, a roll of the dice, or a strategic, aggressive bet that won the day or lost a stake. They were proud of their professionalism.

Along the main streets in cow towns and mining communities across the West, men and women gathered around the tables, the richest and poorest, the prospectors and the real estate developers, the cowboys and the barons, waiting for the turn of the card, the spin of the wheel, and the roll of the dice. In tents and shacks, in saloons and hotels, they eagerly threw their money down. Even in isolated areas of the West, along the railroad construction sites, in remote timber operations, in small mining towns, and on the range, the action was furious.

Folks bet on anything: "Cockfight Tonight: There will be a cockfight in the rear of Stevenson and Walker's Saloon this evening at 6:30 o'clock. Only bettors will be admitted, and all others will be thrown out on their ears." It would not be until 1998 that cockfighting in the state of Arizona was made illegal.

The golden age of the gambler in the West was from the end of the Civil War until the mid-1880s, a time of frontier unrest and unsettled conditions, a time before the domestication of towns and the agitation of antigambling and temperance forces. Tombstone ran the full gamut. Along Allen Street and in other parts of the town, they played poker, keno, euchre, and faro and bet at three-card monte and whist and roulette. They were just learning a game called *vingt et un,* a French import that would flourish in the United States as twenty-one, or blackjack.

Most gamblers played for recreation; some for addiction. For some it was occasional easy money; for others it was habitual losing. Some were predators; others suckers. It was a mania that gripped most of frontier society.

An advertisement in the Silver City, New Mexico, paper declared, "The belligerent portion of the community can find a particularly rampant specimen of the Feline species, usually denominated the 'Tiger,' ready to engage them at all times." The tiger was the bank in the game of faro and, as legend says, it stalked its pleasure-seeking victims.

In Tombstone, the action was intense. The *Epitaph* remarked that "The Call of 'Free Roll' at the keno game, will collect a bigger crowd in 10 minutes than the cry of 'fire' on a windy night."

Faro: The Game of Games

At the Bird Cage Theatre, customers jostled around the faro tables for a game that often lasted no more than thirty seconds. Faro was played on a green oilcloth with the images of thirteen cards of one suit printed on it, ace through king. Although spades were usually depicted, the suits didn't matter since only face value counted. The dealer dealt two cards per turn from a standard deck of fifty-two, and the object was for players to predict which cards would appear.

Bedecked in the usual professional gambler's jet-black frock coat, the dealer used a device called a casekeeper to keep track of the cards that had been played in every deal. He dealt from an open-top, spring-fed box, usually made of German silver.

Although complicated by combination betting, parlaying bets, and other strategies, the game was quick to play, easy to understand, and the odds for the house were slight. The only house advantage was when both the winning and losing cards in a turn came up the same. That was an automatic win for the dealer.

For faro aficionados, the game was extraordinarily intense, often erupting into angry outbursts. It was an argument over a game at the Oriental Saloon in February 1881 that led to a fatal gunfight between two exceptionally slick gamblers, Luke Short and Charlie Storms. A witness to the shooting noted that after the body of Storms was carried off the faro games went on as if nothing had happened.

In gambling halls such as the Bird Cage, ethics took a holiday. The

Faro game in full blast. (Courtesy of the National Archives.)

houses ran games as crooked as they could, short of losing customers or incurring the deadly wrath of the players. The gamblers themselves, often cleverly armed and dangerous, used every deception and ruse known to the gambling world of the 1880s and were, all of them, engaged in pure research to expand the horizons of the science of cheating. As in any area of scientific research and development, some inventors of gambling deception were remarkably ingenious; others ignominious failures. Only a few got rich; many got killed.

One miner wrote later: "The games were as crooked as they dared to be and tended by soft handed, fishy eyed, well dressed, smooth spoken dealers recruited from all over the world; killer gamblers, or tin horns, as we used to call them. . . . they were all out to get the money. If they could get it by clever playing, that was fine, but if it were necessary to run in marked cards on a tenderfoot, or start a quarrel . . . that was fine." There is no evidence to suggest that the atmosphere at the Bird Cage Theatre was any different.

But the great high-roller gamblers and their legendary high-stakes poker games were mostly exaggerations of western lore. Although gambling was ubiquitous in boomtowns such as Tombstone, few fortunes were either won or lost at the tables. The miners who gathered around the roulette wheels and the faro tables did not throw down great amounts of money; they did not have it. The average miner of the day made around twenty dollars a week. The Bird Cage and other gambling establishments relied instead on the volume of citizens who showed up to bring them profits. And across the West, they showed up in great numbers.

Writer Clara Brown, wife of a speculator in Tombstone, put it less than succinctly: "Some of those who participate therein, may leave with heavier pocket-books than were theirs when they went in, but the majority will depart with flat purses. It is an old saying that plenty of gambling is a sure indication of a prosperous camp. Professional gamblers will not remain long where no profits are to be made, and that plenty of money is in circulation is a pretty good sign of abundant yielding mines."

The Longest Game

Old-timers talked about a special poker game at the Bird Cage Theatre. It was, they said, limited to a select company, a high-stakes match in a private room downstairs near the liquor and wine room and the bordello suites. It was a game for the ages, they said, with the minimum buy-in at one thousand dollars, a game that for eight years, five months, and three days did not end. Around the clock, seven players and a house dealer kept the action going, with some of the great names in gambling history—Diamond Jim Brady, Adolph Busch, Bat Masterson, and a host of others—alternating through the years. Sometimes in the telling of the story, the names change and new names are added. Luke Short, one of gambling's greatest artists, is sometimes included as a participant. But Luke left Tombstone in the summer of 1881, before the Bird Cage Theatre opened its doors.

In the longest game, a total of $10 million exchanged hands, the story goes, with the house taking 10 percent. This figure also changes. If the house had taken in $1 million in this game alone, even in the Bird Cage's heyday, the place would have been its own bonanza.

But some say that even years after the Bird Cage closed its doors, years after Wyatt and Sadie supposedly discovered each other's charms in the room next door, years after all of that had ended, the longest game continued—with faint, otherworldly echoes of poker chips in the abandoned room of the closed-up Bird Cage, a suggestive hint of smoke in the air, a sense of tension mixed with frivolity, and a realization that something vital, indeed, was going on.

CHAPTER 12

The Clientele

A writer for the *Epitaph* declared that the Bird Cage was one of the liveliest institutions in the West. It was "the soul of Tombstone at night," he said. "If you wanted to meet a leading lawyer, mine or mill superintendent, the sheriff of the county, the mayor of the city, the editor of any of the daily papers, or any of the bright stars of desperadodom, the chances are that if you penetrated the Bird Cage you would have found them."

In the Bird Cage, men who had taken on the rigors of the West mingled to take on a few of its pleasures.

The Miners

Tombstone was a mining town. The Bird Cage was principally a hangout for miners. One of the prospectors who came to Tombstone in 1881, drawn by the tales circulating all over the West about fabulous riches in the Arizona desert, was Charles Gordes: "I was only a prospector, often dirty, often unshaven, uninteresting to all except a few of my own kind. I

Miners of Spray Shaft, Bunker Hill Mining Company. (Courtesy of the Tombstone
Courthouse State Historic Park.)

plodded out into the desert with a pack mule or two, some grub, perhaps
a partner, and such tools as I felt I would need; and returned months
later, with perhaps a little money to spend, and perhaps not. Most of
my amusement was found in the saloons of the time, in drinking and
gambling. I did both cold-bloodedly and with reason, rather than with
indulgence." Charles was a typical aficionado of the Bird Cage Theatre.

The miners roamed the canyons, draws, and washes, looking for certain
rock formations, certain colors. During a boom, almost any sign of ore was a
reason to file a claim. But in the silver-rich bonanza of Tombstone, the labor
was done mostly by teams of men working for separate companies that had the
equipment necessary for a hard-rock mining operation. They worked as drillers
and drivers, and in their uncertain, hastily erected caverns they risked their lives
daily. George Parsons, who hired on at the Merry Christmas Mine and turned a
hand drill while a fellow worker hammered it with an eight-pound sledge,
wrote in his journal, "More difficult than I imagined to hold drills properly.

One little slip and one's hands, arms or legs might be smashed to a jelly."

As the work progressed, the shafts drove more deeply into the land, a quarter of a mile in some places, and increasing numbers of mule trains hauled the high-grade ore to the stamp mills on the San Pedro River ten miles away. The men faced cave-ins and sudden rushes of water and other perils. They all knew the risks and were willing to take them.

If the miners in the Bird Cage were loud, they had a right to be. The work literally broke some men's bodies; it also broke many men's spirits. Some thrived on a wage of twenty-four dollars a week; others with no regular job lived in primitive shacks and got by on beans, coffee, and a little bacon. They battled malaria and dysentery. One Tombstone miner later wrote, "It was never known whether a miner would ever rise to the surface when the shaky cages were lowered to the four and five hundred levels, through both dry and damp atmosphere and pungent smelling gases."

The drillers and muckers who managed to make it through the ten-hour days uninjured, unbroken, and with a surplus of energy needed respite. Many lost their lives. At a coroner's inquest in Tombstone in November 1882, fellow workers talked about their buddy who was making repairs on top of a cage in the mine shaft when the rickety conveyance unexpectedly lurched. One of the miners, Thomas Stevenson, remembered hearing shouts from the shaft, wheeling around, and seeing James Tully plunge to his death. Life in the mines could be snuffed out in an instant or drained from a man over months or years. The miners needed the lights of Allen Street and the Bird Cage Theatre.

At the Bird Cage, Ed Wittig Jr. said, the miners, regardless of their jobs, all dressed in simple, plain, sometimes grubby clothes. Whether a boss or superintendent or a driller, they came to the theater with little fanfare and without sartorial extravagance.

When a miner was smitten by the charms of a young woman from the other side of Allen Street, the respectable side, he might clean up his act— get a bath, haircut, and shave, attend a few church socials, and buy some new clothes. But often the quest was futile; after all, the odds of any one

Fort Huachuca, Arizona Territory, August 1884. (Courtesy of the Arizona Department of Library, Archives, and Public Records.)

bachelor hooking up with one of the few eligible women were depressingly low. One observer of the Tombstone bachelor ritual commented that the effort was undertaken "for the sake of a new face and the opportunity to learn to curl their little finger around a tea cup in the toniest *fin-de-siècle* manner of the day, when straight whiskey and the Bird Cage was really their calibre."

The Soldiers

For the miners of Tombstone, the Bird Cage was at least close. For the soldiers of Fort Huachuca, the good times were a full day's ride away.

Native Indians called the mountains southwest of Tombstone *Huachuca*, meaning *place of thunder*. Here, where armies of desert clouds, marshaling explosions of light and sound, can assault the landscape with startling and sudden ferocity, the U.S. Army in 1877 built a fort deep in the heart of Apache country. Nestled against the base of the mountains, in a brooding area of hidden caves and failed mines and overgrown with cottonwood and ponderosa pine, Fort Huachuca was home to soldiers who marched on Brown's Parade Field, kept their guns and artillery in wartime order, and prepared to take on the warrior bands that continued to harass small towns and ranches. Here, about fifteen miles from the Mexican border, scouts and lookouts could see clearly in three directions over the San Pedro and Santa Cruz Valleys, could see the trail dust churned up by raiding parties and the smoke and fire left in the aftermath of skirmishes and plunder.

Against such Apache leaders as Victorio, Nana, Charo, and Geronimo, the patrols of hard-bitten noncommissioned officers and young recruits from Huachuca played a deadly game of strike and parry against the war parties. It was Fort Huachuca's 4th U.S. Cavalry Regiment that would finally subdue the daring and clever Geronimo in 1886, a feat that would make the unit famous.

Once a month, the paymaster arrived. Privates received thirteen dollars, corporals fifteen, and sergeants seventeen. Twenty miles away to the southwest, diversions beckoned. Some of the Fort Huachuca soldiers were Civil War veterans who found it impossible to settle down; others were young thugs trying to turn their lives around; some dreamed of conquests and glory in the badlands. Most of them heard the call of Tombstone.

When turned loose, the soldiers swarmed the gaming tables, the bars, and the joy houses. For some, the Bird Cage filled all their needs. For the young horse soldiers, the long nights on the trails and in the barracks were broken by thoughts of Lizette and Crazy Lil and the chance to roll dice and laugh at the comics and hoist a few or many in the nights and lights of Tombstone. Their Army superiors, realizing the isolation of the camp, began to allow three-day passes. And thus the pleasure trek was made real—most of a day's ride to Tombstone by horseback, a day's good time and a period to recover, and most of a day's ride back to the fort.

"What money the soldiers did not throw away on women, whiskey, and the gambling tables," one of Tombstone's residents remembered, "was generally stolen from them by . . . harpies." As they returned to the fort, a sufficient number were organized into a squad of military police for a return to Tombstone to round up their missing buddies.

Ranch Hands and Cowboys

Although the appellation Cowboy had taken on a singular connotation to the people of Tombstone as the group allied with the Clantons in their feud with the Earps, the word also began to refer to an increasing number of individuals in southern Arizona who made their living in the cattle business. As the silver bonanza attracted increasing numbers of people to Tombstone, the ranchers and meat-market owners began to profit from the increased demand for beef. It was one thing to feast on the meat of antelope, which were plentiful in the area; it was another to get a fresh beefsteak.

The cattle business in Arizona, almost totally dependent on markets outside the territory, now had a much stronger local outlet. For the Arizona cowboy, with cattle bringing about twelve dollars a head, prospects were improving.

All across the Southwest, cattle rustling was part of the business. Back and forth across the Mexican border, gangs hustled cattle, fought off enemy gangs, battled with Apache raiders, carried on disputes with claim jumpers, repaired equipment without a good stock of tools, worried about sources of water, and protected the herds against bears and other potential threats, all the time trying to accomplish the work necessary to feed, protect, and market the herds.

Henry Clay Hooker, a rancher near Tombstone, said his fellow cowboys came from all walks of life. The one prerequisite: that they be tough. "We take a man here and ask no questions. We know when he throws a saddle on his horse whether he understands his business or not. He may be a minister back-slidin', or a banker savin' his last lung, or a train robber on vacation—we don't care. All we care about is, will they stand the gaff?" Sixty hours in the saddle in one stretch with a herd that wants to stampede, said Hooker, separated the fit from the unfit.

The typical trail hand was described by a newspaperman: "His dress consists of a flannel shirt with a handkerchief encircling his neck. . . . his head is covered with a sombrero, which is a Mexican hat with a low crown and a brim of mammoth dimensions. He generally wears a revolver on each side, which he will use with as little hesitation on a man as on a wild animal."

If it was difficult for the general population of Tombstone to tell an honest rancher from a rustler, it was because the distinctions themselves were often blurred. Often, men would work both sides. John Pleasant Gray, a man involved in the Arizona cattle business, wrote of the McLaurys in his memoirs: "They may have harbored passing rustlers at their ranch, but what rancher did not? and it would have been little of a man who would have turned away any traveler in that land of long trails and hard going."

Although many of the cowhands in the vicinity of Tombstone hung out at the town of Charleston, the home of the Clantons, and in Galeyville, on the eastern slope of the Chiricahua Mountains, many mixed with the miners and others at the Bird Cage. There were prostitutes and gambling and liquor in Charleston and Galeyville, but there was nothing like the Bird Cage.

In Charleston and Galeyville, the men could get gambling, liquor, and women, but the Bird Cage, with its entertainment and higher-class prostitutes, beckoned any and all men looking for excitement. And whether the men were cowhands from local ranches or rustlers fresh from a raid into Mexico, the entrepreneurs in Tombstone, especially those of the Bird Cage Theatre, did not discriminate. For all patrons, their money was good, whether American dollars or Mexican pesos.

CHAPTER 13

"The Chinese Must Go"

When the city of Tucson razed many of the old downtown buildings during a massive urban renewal program in the 1980s, archaeologists from the University of Arizona discovered many ornate nineteenth-century glass opium pipes still undamaged. According to a Chinese woman who lived in Tombstone, Doc Holliday regularly used opium. In those days, opium was a treatment for tuberculosis and Doc suffered from the disease. The use of the drug was not illegal. If many of the customers at the Bird Cage Theatre seemed somewhat high even before they hit the bottle, the poppy plant may have had something to do with it.

Although most of the Chinese people in Tombstone were hard workers in the mines or on the railroad, many of the town's citizens had little use for the Chinese themselves. Of the many offensive sobriquets aimed at the Chinese, the word *Celestials*, from Celestial Empire, was perhaps the most common and least derisive. Anti-Chinese sentiment in Arizona was reaching fire-red hysteria in the 1880s. One miner, writing to his family about his search for riches in Arizona, talked about "yellow-skinned, pig-tailed chinamen who smoked opium pipes in a cave. . . . Just a hell-hole of lost souls."

Almost as soon as the California gold rush began in 1849, Chinese workers, especially from the poverty-racked coastal province of Canton, began to arrive in California, a place they called Gam-San (Gold Mountain, in Cantonese). They fanned out across California and into other western states, willing to work for wages well below those paid to other workers.

At the end of the American Civil War, Chinese workers were also recruited for construction of the transcontinental railroad to make up for a labor shortage. The men received ten to twenty dollars per month, a food allowance or rations of rice, fish, beef, pork, and vegetables, and some eating utensils. Although the workers furnished their own bedding, the railroad was responsible for providing waterproof quarters. The Chinese laborers were segregated from the other workers.

The needs of the railroad thus opened up further opportunities for the Chinese, although the American West was becoming a more hostile place as their numbers increased. By the time the Southern Pacific Railroad reached Tucson on March 20, 1880, it had been responsible for the largest settlement of Chinese laborers in Arizona Territory, including more than eleven hundred individuals in Pima County.

As word of the effectiveness of Chinese laborers spread, the owners of Arizona's copper mines also began to use them extensively. It was profitable. They were cheap and reliable, and if occasionally a few disappeared, few questions were asked.

Nevertheless, if Chinese workers were good for management, they were not good for other potential workers unwilling to do backbreaking labor for a pittance. Newspapers in Arizona openly attacked this new segment of the population. In Prescott an editorialist noted in 1869, "Three more Chinamen arrived here during the week and have gone to work. There are now four of them, which is quite enough." The *Star* ran an editorial in 1879 portraying them as "an ignorant, filthy, leprous horde." When the railroad companies originally brought Chinese laborers to the United States, they never intended them to become permanent members of American society, assuming they would return to China. While many

Chinese did return to their homeland, others remained and became members of communities across the West.

Like other cultural groups new to the United States, the Chinese clung to their customs and lived mostly in distinct areas. Several hundred were attracted to Tombstone's silver boom and settled in an area on the outskirts of Tombstone

With its honeycombed network of underground tunnels and dens for gambling and smoking, the Chinese section was mysterious and fearsome, yet alluring. As opium's sweet odors mixed with the sounds of a culture far removed from the Arizona desert, fascination mixed with repulsion in the larger community. Who were these people? Did they eat roasted puppy dog with caterpillar sauce and sip worm chowder? Who were these people who refused to dress like others in the mining community, who imported their clothes, who were able, it seemed, to live on almost nothing?

The Chinese worked as launderers, cooks, gardeners, and woodcutters at very low wages. A man named Sam Hing ran the Bird Cage Laundry next door to the Bird Cage Theatre. Some of them engaged in truck farming in nearby Fairbank and provided fresh produce for both Tombstone and Benson.

The Chinese seldom patronized town businesses, managing to import much of their clothing and food from China. Leaning on each other, they survived in this foreign desert wilderness through grit and guile and through a willingness to work long and hard.

In Tombstone's Chinese community all roads, it seemed, led to China Mary. She arrived in Tombstone in late 1879 or early 1880. Nobody knew her real name or much about her past. When she married Ah Lum, master of the Chinese Masonic Lodge, the two controlled whatever power the Chinese wielded in Tombstone. In her elaborate brocaded clothes and exotic jewelry, China Mary became the principal contact between the Chinese and Tombstone's town leaders. She placed Chinese workers in jobs in the town, often helped the sick, injured, and hungry, and even loaned money. She ran everything from a well-stocked store of Chinese

Quong Lee opened the Can Can Restaurant on Allen Street. (Courtesy of the Tombstone Courthouse State Historic Park.)

delicacies and artworks to a gambling operation in hidden rooms. She also, it is said, supplied most of the opium to Tombstone's dens.

The Racist Impulse

Chinese workers across the West found themselves facing the increasing hostility and resentment of their hosts. As early as 1880, a group of Tombstone residents, led by *Tombstone Epitaph* editor John Clum, had banded together to hold mass meetings in the streets to demand the exclusion of the Chinese from Tombstone. The *Epitaph* reported, "A committee of ten was appointed to convey the sentiments of the meetings to the despised Mongolians. . . ."

When several Chinese laborers were hired to work on the construction of the new courthouse, the *Epitaph* railed: "We suggest that white men desiring employment present themselves in an offer to relieve the imported labor, and thus leave no excuse for its retention. The *Epitaph* is heartily opposed to Chinese labor when made competitive with white labor, and its columns are always open for the condemnation of the employment of the former." Like other racist and nativist groups throughout United States history, the anti-Chinese element in Tombstone found sport in starting bonfires in the streets and shouting racial slurs.

Even though many citizens were not fond of the presence of the Chinese, whom they distrusted and feared, many felt that compulsory ejection would violate treaty laws between the United States and China and would lead to bloodshed on Tombstone's streets if ever enforced. Indeed, many of the Chinese, not inclined to be cowed by bonfires, purchased pistols, and as one woman wrote, seemed "disposed to defend their rights."

As some of the boomtowns in the West busted and as jobs on the railroads decreased, it was easy for some workers to blame the despised Chinese for declining wages and other economic ills. Although the Chinese composed a tiny number of the nation's total inhabitants, Congress reacted in 1882 by passing the Chinese Exclusion Act, the first significant law restricting immigration into the United States. The statute suspended Chinese immigration for ten years and declared the Chinese ineligible for naturalization. Chinese workers already in the country challenged the constitutionality of the discriminatory act, but their efforts failed.

In April 1882, in the neighborhood of Crittenden, Arizona, one of the stops of the Atchison, Topeka & Santa Fe Railroad, some of the contractors and superintendents in charge of railroad construction were nearly lynched because they were using increasing numbers of Chinese laborers. On the night of April 23, a drunken mob, wielding pick handles and shovels, drove a group of Chinese workers like a flock of sheep to a siding, where they were told to take the next train out of the area. J. D. Scott, in charge of construction work in the area, was swung up on a telegraph pole, fitted with a rope for his neck, and threatened with extinction if he did not promise to refrain from using "Celestials" in the area. Scott agreed.

By 1886, the *Epitaph* called for the creation of an organization to drive the Chinese out of town. The paper helped raise five thousand dollars to set up a white-operated steam laundry. The *Epitaph* sounded the call. "The Chinese are the least desired immigrants who have ever sought the United States," editor John Clum began. "The most we can do is to insist that he is a heathen, a devourer of soup made of the fragrant juice of the rat, filthy, disagreeable, and undesirable generally, an encumbrance that we do not know how to get rid of, but whose tribe we have determined shall not increase in this part of the world."

But the anti-Chinese prejudice came with a practical price. An editorialist, countering some of Clum's rantings, pointed out that there was in the southwestern desert a definite shortage of good white help. Some of the Arizona citizens who, in fits of racial hysteria, discharged Chinese workers later found that the replacement workers were neither as dependable nor as inexpensive. "To expect a business man for the good of his race to put up with the vagaries of a drunkard, who works when it suits him, while he expects twice as much as a Chinaman, is asking a little too much." Race agitators who wanted to replace Chinese laborers, he said, "should conduct themselves in a manner as least as decently as "the heathen, of whose vices they are so fond of prating."

Xenophobia on the Playbill

The Bird Cage Theatre added to the racial tensions. A number of the anti-Chinese leaders frequented the Bird Cage and began to use its facilities to spread the cause. Marshaling song and satire, the honkytonk proprietors gave special performances designed to spread the anti-Chinese gospel. One *Tombstone Epitaph* reporter was thoroughly amused by the production called *The Chinese Must Go*, comparing its humor to that of Mark Twain.

However, the heartiest amusement that night did not come from searing wit or comedic nuance—it came from a lowly burro. In the last scene of the last act, a Chinese laundryman is put on a burro with his portable stove, dirty clothes, and other personal effects, to be escorted out of town. "For some reason or other," the newspaperman said, "the burro preferred remaining on stage. He could not be led off, neither could he be backed off. Like the Rock of Gibraltar, he had come to stay, and stay he did. . . . His burroship had evidently joined the pro-Chinese crowd."

A number of Tombstone's politicians, civic leaders, and troublemakers did follow the lead of John Clum and the *Epitaph* to form a nasty xenophobic coalition dedicated to the expulsion of the Chinese. The Anti-Chinese League, they called themselves. A reporter from the *Epitaph* attended one of the league's meetings. And there, employed for the evening, were performers from the Bird Cage, spicing the disjointed oratory and racist balderdash with rousing, lusty entertainment. From the spirited invective came tactics to deal with the Chinese, and plans for intimidation and economic boycott to force Tombstone residents to cease hiring the undesirables from the Far East. The pronouncements were swift and incisive: "Colonel Herring has a family of women who should do their own work";

The Cochise Hardware Company is "velly bad"; "members of the League have no business with the Cochise County bank."

Although the league eventually claimed about eight hundred members, the effort to drive the Chinese residents from Tombstone was generally unsuccessful. The nativist impulse was far from universally supported. When the movement began in 1882, the Chinese represented about 4 percent of the community; in 1900 it was 3 percent.

In the years following approval of the Chinese Exclusion Act and other anti-Chinese policies, many Chinese workers and their families left the United States for Mexico. Many signed on as laborers for the Colorado River Land Company, an American-run enterprise established to build an irrigation system in the Valle de Mexicali.

By 1927 civil unrest exploded in northern Mexico over control of gambling and prostitution rings. Alarm over Chinese participation in organized crime led to the Movimiento Anti-Chino in the late 1920s, a government-sanctioned wave of anti-immigrant sentiment that swept the country and led to the torture and murder of hundreds of Chinese in northern Mexico. Although the Mexican government never enacted legislation equivalent to the Chinese Exclusion Act in the United States, the violence had the same effect. Thousands of Chinese fled Mexico across the United States border and made arrangements for sailing to China.

On a day in 1931, a group of twenty individuals of Chinese descent, escaping from the persecution, stopped for a brief time in Tombstone. A photographer gathered them together and took a picture. They stood in front of the Bird Cage Theatre.

CHAPTER 14

The Joe and Minnie Show

B illy Hutchinson's ownership of the Bird Cage ended in 1883.
It all had to do with water. In 1881, miners had struck water
amidst the silver. At first, it seemed like good news, an additional bonanza for use in the town and for its mills. The water
in Tombstone's mines, however, was far too abundant, and by 1883 it was
evident that tremendous pumping would be necessary to keep the mines
operating. At first, the two largest mines invested over $350,000 to install
pumps to raise 2.5 million gallons a day. It was not enough. When the
shafts continued to flood, the owners installed the most modern pumps of
the day to siphon off more than 6 million gallons a day. In succeeding days
and months, the land gave up more and more water, less and less silver.
Although Billy Hutchinson loved the Bird Cage, he realized that much of
his clientele would be moving out. He did also. He had run the Bird Cage
for less than two years.

For a time the Bird Cage was without a proprietor and, except for
special benefits, closed down. Joe Bignon, variety entrepreneur and clog-
dancer extraordinaire, became its savior.

The Education of a Frontier Stage Performer

From his earliest years, Joe Bignon had yearned to become an entertainer. A runaway at age twelve, he became a member of Pendergast, Miller, and Kingsley's Minstrels, learning the blackface routines that characterized early American minstrel entertainment. He was also a member of the Grant Brothers, one of the variety acts that featured clogging. As with many young stage entertainers, Joe found the lure of wanderlust irresistible—that peripatetic life of new sounds and sights.

He joined a traveling comedy team called Brewster, Skirrow, and Bignon, then moved on with an Australian circus outfit. After settling down for a short time to form a theater partnership in Wisconsin, he became the proprietor of Miller's Hall in Chicago and then opened Bignon's Varieties in Luddington, Michigan. He later moved west and landed in Tucson, where he assumed a partnership in the Park Theatre, a saloon-variety hall that had begun to attract attention as both a place of legitimate stage productions and, to some, a mysterious sin-hole destined to lead the town toward a Gomorrah-like doom.

Joe showed off his clog dancing as well as his "Ethiopian acting" skits in blackface. He cavorted on stage like a gymnast. He performed one of his favorite acts in a full-body monkey suit complete with a long tail bearing a hook at its end. The climax of each performance came when he attached the hook to a wire that was stretched between two fake palm trees and swung out over the audience. Not surprisingly, he once got the tail entangled with the wire and plunged into the lap of a spectator. After assessing that the fall had caused no injury, Joe stayed in character, leaping up, scratching his head, and bounding up behind the curtain and out of sight.

Joe was soon on the move again, leaving Tucson and the Park Theatre to manage San Francisco's Theatre Comique at Pine and Kearney Streets for several years. In January 1886, he returned to Arizona—to revitalize the

The principal mode of public transportation. (Courtesy of the Center for Southwest Research, University of New Mexico.)

Bird Cage Theatre. For a time, he called it the Elite Theatre. He redecorated the place, installed new seats, used his connections in the show world to hire an unusually diverse group of entertainers, changed the program often, and offered his own skills, along with those of his wife, to the Bird Cage scene.

The Fabulous Big Minnie

Joe's wife had much to offer. She became one of Tombstone's most familiar entertainers—Big Minnie. "Six-feet tall and 230 pounds of loveliness in pink tights," she was described by a local writer. Beside her somewhat diminutive husband, Minnie towered. She sang, played the piano, did ballet skits, and on occasion acted as bouncer at the Bird Cage.

To drunks who caused trouble, Minnie was anything but lovely. She would wrap her arm around a troublemaker's neck and toss him in the street. Although Big Minnie was tough, she still had a long way to go to match the reputations of other notable barmaids and brothel bouncers across the West. In Butte, Montana, for example, a madam calling herself Dirty Mouth Jean Sorenson earned her sobriquet by using strings of epithets and discourse more foul, it was said, than any language heard from the mouth of any woman west of Paris. Jean kept a long club, which she claimed was a petrified walrus penis, behind the bar to keep her clientele in line.

Compared to Dirty Mouth Jean, Minnie was unusually friendly, loved the action of the Bird Cage, and sympathized with the down and outs. She and Joe made the Bird Cage rock. They hired magicians, ventriloquists, trapeze acts, high-kicking dancers, and even a troupe who specialized in the circus feat of human pyramids.

Under Joe and Minnie's inspired direction, the place took off to even greater heights of bawdy acclaim. Changing programs at least once a week, Joe introduced Tombstone to an unmatched array of variety and circus performers, mostly out of San Francisco. They set up a dramatic stock company for performances of such entertainments as *One Night in a Barroom* and *The Irish Nightingale*.

Many of the new entertainers brought with them a shady past. One Professor Ricardo, carrying a billing as "Wonder of Wonders in Feats of Legerdemain and Hindoo Juggling, Light and Heavy Balancing, Sword Swallowing and Fire-eating," was actually an Army deserter from Fort Huachuca named Edmund Don Loder. Although Professor Ricardo was a hit with Bird Cage audiences, Loder was plucked from the stage one night by the county sheriff and carried off to jail.

The year 1887 was busy at the Bird Cage. One night it was John Crawford in the trick tumbling contortions act he called "Fun in a Parlor"; the next night it was the Ulm Sisters and their "Tyrolian warbling" or, to most observers, simple yodeling. And not very good yodeling. One night, as the audience did its very best to drown out the onstage sounds of the Ulms, the house did its best to assist its performers. "It is respectfully suggested," said the impresario, "that a good many persons attended the performance for the pleasure of hearing the singing, and that it is the height of rudeness and ill manners to laugh and talk in a boisterous

Minnie Bignon, 1886. (Courtesy of Tombstone Courthouse State Historic Park.)

manner, at least during that portion of the programme." The rebuke to the audience had little effect.

In 1888, travelers to Tombstone reported that Bignon had turned the Bird Cage into one of the liveliest attractions they had seen anywhere, and that between the hours of 8 P.M. and 5 A.M. it rocked as no other. The place continued to offer the same sensual delights as it did during Billy Hutchinson's management. It was still almost entirely patronized by men looking for women, booze, gambling, and variety acts. But under Joe Bignon, the Bird Cage seemed to reach an even more feverish beat.

Sometimes the riotous entertainment erupted almost beyond Bignon's control. Starved for diversion, clouded by booze, the clientele was always on the edge, unfettered by the usual restraints of polite society. Amidst the noise, the delirium, and the near-naked ladies, passions rose, tempers boiled, excitement reigned, and shots from small-arms weapons even zinged around the place.

On May 11, 1889, the following occurrence went down: An intoxicated reveler, a woodchopper from the Dragoon Mountains, offended by the fact that bartender Charley Keene asked him for an additional nickel for his next shot of Mumm's Extra Dry, brandished a pistol. A reporter for the *Prospector* completed the tale: "Charley looked at the man and he had his eyes fixed on Charley. At this moment, Mrs. Bignon entered and Charley asked her to stay there while he went after Bob Hatch to put the man out. She answered that she would put him out, and suiting the action to the words proceeded to put the objectionable visitor out the front door." But on the way to jail, he broke free from his captors, began exchanging shots outside the Bird Cage with the officers, was subdued a second time, and was finally incarcerated.

Sometimes the trouble involved no men at all. The Tombstone *Prospector* reported, "A little episode not down on the bills occurred at the close of the programme last Saturday night at the Bird Cage. A couple of female attachés had a hair pulling contest for a few seconds, which but for the promptness of Joe Bignon, might have ended in a general row."

Despite the Bird Cage's disorderly reputation, Joe and Minnie on some occasions sent members of their troupe to make special appearances at Schieffelin Hall. Here, on the stage where opera and other classical forms of artistic endeavor flourished, the Bird Cage performers could reach a more polite audience. The shows were mutually satisfying: The audiences at the Schieffelin could enjoy the Bird Cage talent free from extracurricular gambling, boozing, and whoring; and the Bird Cage singers and actors could strut their stuff liberated from the confines of a seedy variety hall. One pledge was part of the arrangement: The Bird Cage troupe in this setting would provide entertainment "of a moral tone and first class in every particular."

Despite the economic downturn of Tombstone and the growing dislocation of many of its citizens, despite the uncertainties that almost everyone in the town was experiencing in those days, Joe and Minnie had created a haven. They had resurrected a house of pleasure and good times for a boomtown that, unfortunately, was soon to go bust.

The Tragedy of Bird Cage Mollie and Buckskin Frank

He was a gunslinger and gambler with a past that will likely remain clouded and mysterious; she was a Bird Cage dancer and floozy. The dapper but dangerous Frank Leslie had killed several men in his storied life. But then he killed Mollie.

He had drifted into Tombstone with the hundreds of others in 1880 looking for riches and excitement. A flashy charmer, intelligent and arrogant, the epitome of the Western showman on the make, the smooth-talking, blue-eyed Leslie took a bartending job in a saloon in the Cosmopolitan Hotel. A year later, when the building succumbed to one of the town's frequent fires, Frank mixed drinks at the Oriental Saloon, as elegant a watering spot, some said, as any in the mining towns of the West.

The Dandy

Frank Leslie worked at his image. Small, wiry, at first wearing buckskins and later a Prince Albert coat, sporting checkered pants and a fancy shirt decorated with pearl studs, his boots shined to a mirror finish, an impeccably curled mustache completing the dashing appearance, Leslie was one of Tombstone's dandies, a charmer and scoundrel whose life was a mad chase from one gambling hall to another, from one woman to another. The *Epitaph* remarked about Leslie: "When sober he is gentlemanly and courteous, but when drinking is disagreeable and always ready to use his pistol."

The mad chase that was Frank's life sometimes led to violence and Frank was ever ready for it. Always looking for an edge, the legendary gunman hired a Tombstone silversmith named Ed Williams to fashion a silver slotted plate to fit on the right side of his belt. Frank also had him attach a knob on his revolver to fit into the slot on the silver plate. The gunfighter could then fire from the hip without drawing his gun from the holster. He could unerringly hit a fly from thirty feet, the boys around Frank claimed. Few shooters were anxious to tangle with Buckskin Frank. Wyatt Earp reportedly remarked that Frank was the only man he had ever encountered who was as fast on the draw as Doc Holliday.

In June 1880, Frank began to make amorous advances toward May Killeen, the gorgeous, black-haired wife of Mike Killeen, bartender at Lowry and Archer's saloon. One evening that month, while tending bar, Mike not only served drinks to Frank Leslie but also served him a warning about his advances toward May. Leslie told his friend George Perine that Killeen had threatened to kill both May and himself (Leslie) if they showed up at a town ball that night.

Later in the evening, a friend notified Killeen that Leslie and May had indeed been seen at the dance. The enraged bartender stormed out of the hotel and went looking for the couple. He found them at the Cosmopolitan Hotel. The explosion of gunshots resulted in the predictable. Killeen lay dying. He had managed to crease Leslie's skull with a bullet but had taken a mortal shot to the chest. In a deathbed statement, Killeen wasn't sure who had actually fired the fatal shot. John Clum, attempting to gather some perspective on the matter, declared: "The causes which led to these desperate results found their origins in domestic infelicity and the blind, restless passions of love and jealousy."

In the days following, both Leslie and Perine were arrested for Killeen's killing while law enforcement officials began sorting out the various stories to try to determine the killer. When it was revealed that Killeen had stalked Buckskin Frank and had threatened to kill him, and when investigators seemed hopelessly divided over the basic fact of whether it was Perine or Leslie who had pulled the trigger, the charges were dropped.

A few days after Killeen's interment on Boot Hill, Frank and May wasted no time in getting on with their lives. Undeterred by the whispers and inferences, they got married.

In November 1882, another gunman went after Buckskin Frank—Billy Claiborne. Young Billy's first claim to infamy had been his involvement with the Clantons and the McLaurys and the members of the infamous Cowboy group. Hot-tempered, cocky, and looking for excitement, Billy had eagerly joined up with the outlaws, a group perfectly matching his temperament and ambition.

The young miscreant liked to be called Billy the Kid, a signal to everyone in the Tombstone area of his pretensions. Indeed, a writer for the *San Francisco Chronicle,* reporting on events in Arizona's new boomtown, actually confused Claiborne with the famous Billy the Kid from New Mexico, whose dubious exploits in the Lincoln County War had made *The New York Times* and other papers across the county. A writer to the *Chronicle* tried to bring enlightenment: "You paper men have got them confounded. He is out on the range south of Tucson to get out of the way of the officers who want him for his last shooting scrape." In late October 1881, Billy Claiborne and his friends the Clantons and McLaurys did battle with the Earps and friends at the O.K. Corral. But on that fateful day, Billy did not distinguish himself. As the shooting started, a bullet ripped through one of his pants legs and he quickly disappeared inside a building. Billy was anxious to get that unfortunate and embarrassing encounter behind him. What better way to redeem himself than taking down the symbol of machismo in Tombstone, Buckskin Frank Leslie!

Billy picked the spot for the confrontation—Frank's home turf, the

Oriental Saloon, where he was attending bar. After downing a few shots poured by the target himself, Billy began to insult Frank. After warning the young man to behave, Frank grabbed him by the shirt and tossed him roughly out of the saloon onto Allen Street. According to some witnesses in the bar, Billy yelled back to Frank, "See you later." Frank, it is said, replied, "While I'm in Tombstone you can see me any time."

Ed Wittig Jr., the son of the orchestra leader at the Bird Cage who was working as a barber in a shop across the street from the Oriental Saloon, saw Billy, Winchester in hand, hiding behind a peanut stand at the corner of Fifth Street. When the barber pointed out the lurker on the street to a friend, the man, knowing of Claiborne's designs on Frank, raced across the street to warn the prey of "Billy the Kid."

These were the moments for which Frank Leslie lived. He calmly, deliberately, rolled a cigarette, lit it, and checked his guns. He was prepared for battle.

An eyewitness later said: "Leslie went out the back way and came around the front of the building with his six-shooter out and when Claiborne saw him, he began to raise the rifle, but Leslie was the quicker and dropped Billy the Kid, whose shot went off into the ground at Leslie's feet." One observer noted that the infamous gunfighter had not even lost the light of his cigarette in the deadly fracas.

Billy Claiborne was not mourned in Tombstone. In his diary George Parsons noted that the Kid, a notorious "bad egg," had been killed and had gone to hell.

Frank and the Silhouette Girl

The marriage between Frank and May lasted seven years, despite May's claims that Frank frequently beat and choked her, that he was usually drunk, and that he had taken up with Birdie Woods, one of the red-light girls on Allen Street. May said he spent numerous nights holed up in the Bird Cage, gambling and carousing.

Buckskin Frank Leslie. (Courtesy of the Arizona Department of Library, Archives, and Public Records.)

Frank's transgressions did not end there. He reputedly thought noth-ing of standing May up against their house on several occasions to shoot bullets around her profile. "Stand perfectly still, my dear," Frank would say, and then rapidly surround her form with bullets. Only after her outline was finished would she be free to step out of the bullet silhouette so that Frank could fill in the details of eyes, nose, and mouth. This unusual target practice (perhaps Frank considered it a peculiar kind of artistry) earned the unfortunate woman the sobriquet of "the silhouette girl." The abused May, whom a friend described as living "in constant fear of Leslie," finally sued for divorce. Frank did not contest it.

Despite the bizarre clouds of his past, Frank did achieve a degree of civic standing. For a time, he was a mounted customs inspector along the U.S.–Mexico border, helping to stem the tide of smuggled Mexican products and Chinese laborers coming into the country. He was given a deputy sheriff appointment and often served as a member of posses assembled by the Earp brothers. He worked as a civilian guide and courier for General George Crook's forces chasing Geronimo's Apaches in the mountains east and south of Tombstone. He even served as a sergeant at arms of a local Democratic Party convention.

Deputy Sheriff Billy Breakenridge once said of Frank: "He had a fine voice and sang well, told good stories, never complained, never tired; in short, he was the life of the party." Another Tombstone resident added, "He was quite an agreeable man when he wished to be, having a good voice and a fondness for singing, and being an interesting conversationalist." All of this when he wasn't peppering bullets around the form of his female prop.

The Bird Cage Theatre was Frank Leslie's nest. Here in this one single haven, within the walls of this fabulous honkytonk, Leslie found most of his beloved vices. Here was his spot, choked with smoke, flowing with liquor, shaking with the beats of raucous music and frenetic entertainers and the shouts and screams of winners and losers, and fevered with the sights of loose amours. Here, he could strut his stuff with other gamblers and gunslingers and womanizers. Here, he held court, spinning to wide-eyed, if sometimes dubious, listeners his fabulous stories of wide-open frontier towns, of Indians on the run, of bad men brought down, of ladies seduced, and of stakes games won and lost.

As the Bird Cage Theatre gave rise to many colorful legends, most of them not necessarily verifiable but told and retold for generations, one of the stories had Buckskin Frank and his friend "Uncle" Dave Adams enjoying the show from one of the Bird Cage boxes. With a stunningly beautiful vixen showing off her fine qualities from the stage, a man draped one of his legs over the railing, an action that the unpredictable Leslie took as an impertinent gesture. Enraged, Buckskin yelled for the man to take in his leg. No response in the din of the theater. "Take in yer leg," Buckskin shouted again. Still no response. Buckskin then nonchalantly drew his gun, aimed at the man's shoe, and with one shot blasted the heel into oblivion. The leg, amazingly spared from serious injury or obliteration, retreated quickly from view, never to return.

Blonde Mollie of the Bird Cage

Frank fell for several girls at the Bird Cage; he fell hardest for a song and dance girl named Mollie Williams. Mollie, along with Gertie, The Gold Dollar, was one of Tombstone's most striking blondes (most residents assumed that both had used peroxide to achieve the desired results). The alluring Mollie had been close to violence several times in her young life. In May 1884, as the twenty-two-year-old worked as a cook in nearby Fairbank, she came within ten feet of a street shooting that took the life of a man named W. J. Mason. Mollie testified at a Justice of the Peace inquest: "I walked up to the corner of the adobe and I heard a remark, 'You are a God damn liar and you haven't got the nerve to shoot.'" The speaker of those words, W. J. Mason, was promptly shot and killed.

Mollie later took a job as a dancer at the Bird Cage and became one of the many colorful women of Tombstone's red-light district who dragged their ruffled dresses along the dust-covered boards and through the swinging doors of the establishments on Allen Street. She began to occupy one of the notorious cribs inhabited by the soiled doves near the Bird Cage. Although some claim to remember her singing duets of such favorites as "Golden Slippers" with Bird Cage proprietor Billy Hutchinson when she first took a job at the honkytonk, Billy had sold the Bird Cage long before the time Mollie arrived.

Mollie took the last names of several men with whom she lived for periods of time. In 1889 she was with E. L. Bradshaw, an individual who had recently killed a man, it was said, over an argument involving the colors of a shirt. T. J. Waters, a man who had prospected and shared a cabin with Bradshaw, apparently bought a blue-and-black plaid shirt one morning and marched forth onto the streets of Tombstone expecting envious glances and cheerful compliments. He got derision. Friends looked at the plaid shirt and came forth with good-natured but disparaging comments. In a deposition given many years later, Wyatt Earp recalled that "everybody was making fun of it. . . ."

The sartorial criticism began to infuriate Waters. As the day wore on and as Waters began to consume copious amounts of liquor, whatever patience he had with his critics had long since vanished. At one point, the *Tombstone Epitaph* reported, Waters railed: "I'll knock down the first son of a bitch that says anything about my shirt again."

Bradshaw turned out to be the next person. In the back room of Corrigan's Saloon, Bradshaw made a somewhat innocuous remark about the shirt and Waters pounded him in the head. Within a few minutes the confrontation turned deadly serious. Bradshaw, known as one of Waters's best friends, shot him four times.

As many other red-light beauties had done before her, Mollie fell for the charms of Buckskin Frank. Witty, worldly Frank cruised through Allen Street's lady population with nearly unmatched savoir faire. When Frank and Mollie began to see each other regularly, Bradshaw strategically turned his affections to another of the Bird Cage performers, piano player Ollie Callister.

But soon after the "bad-color shirt" killing, Bradshaw himself turned up dead one morning in a local mine dump, his head bashed in. Although rumors for a time had it that a thug known as Peter the Brute had committed the crime, Peter seemed to have an alibi. For a time, the name of Buckskin Frank headed the suspect list. The murder, however, was never solved.

For the second time since he arrived in Tombstone, Frank Leslie was now free to carry on a relationship with a woman in mourning. He decided to take the buxom Mollie away from all of this, away from the Bird Cage, to a ranch about thirty miles from Tombstone in the Swisshelm Mountains that his boss at the Oriental, Milt Joyce, had turned over to him. Frank was not a rancher but he had agreed to keep up the place they called The Magnolia.

Mollie would no longer be a Bird Cage dove, the addled Frank decided. No, Frank would take her away from this degradation. But when Mollie agreed to leave Tombstone for the ranch, she unwittingly traded the Bird Cage for another cage, one that seemed to get progressively more confining. With his mind and mood swings increasingly clouded by alcohol, Frank Leslie headed further into a downward spiral of confusion and paranoia. He began to insist that Mollie stay mostly at the ranch. When she expressed a desire to go to town if only to visit old friends at the Bird Cage, Frank would lose control. The two would fight, he would beg forgiveness, and the cycle would start all over again. On the porch of the house in the Swisshelms, night after night, Frank and Mollie, on the brink of tragedy, drank and argued.

Frank had hired a teenager named James Neil to take care of many of the chores around the small ranch. A middling cowpuncher with a worshipful regard for the renowned Leslie, young Neil was known somewhat derisively around Tombstone as Six-Shooter Jim because of his unrestrained male braggadocio and his weird, fanciful tales of outdrawing slick gunslingers.

Not surprisingly, Jim and Mollie became friends. He was, after all, about the only human other than Frank Leslie who now occupied her life. When Frank began to suspect Mollie and Jim of sexual peccadilloes, the atmosphere at the Swisshelms retreat became dangerously charged.

On the night of July 10, 1889, between nine and ten, it all exploded. A drunken Leslie found James Neil sitting on the porch with Mollie. He cracked. Stomping around the porch flailing an ivory-handled pistol, he screamed at the two. The terrified Mollie tried to run. Frank shot her down. He then turned to Six-Shooter Jim and blasted him point-blank. At

155

first, in the crush of confusion and chaos, Neil didn't realize that his idol had shot him. And then he saw blood on his shirt. Frank calmly shot him again. Mollie died; Frank thought that Neil was also dead. He was not.

After regaining consciousness, the wounded Neil, blood-spattered from wounds in his chest and arms, staggered in the early morning hours to the Reynolds ranch in a nearby valley, where neighbors bandaged his wounds. LeRoy Moody, a worker at the ranch, later recalled that a disheveled and almost incoherent Frank Leslie showed up at the ranch a short time later shouting obscenities, saying he was looking for James Neil who had killed his Blonde Mollie of the Bird Cage. Frank must have returned to the scene of the crime and found Neil gone. Moody said Leslie had shouted that "he was bound to follow him and find him if it took him all his life." Leslie did not find Neil. Moody had hidden him in the chicken coop.

Frank evidently realized he was in a bad hole, but probably thought he had better get his story to the sheriff before Neil could be heard from. But the witness, on his part, realized his own danger if Leslie should find him, so he made all haste to reach Tombstone and place himself under the protection of the law. With the help of men on the ranch, Neil reached Tombstone and told his story.

Cochise County deputies, led by Sheriff John Slaughter, began what many thought would be a futile search for Leslie. Some figured he would have fled to Mexico or New Mexico. But surprisingly the four-man posse found him along one of the roads leading to Tombstone. Buckskin Frank Leslie was led to town and wrestled into a cell. A Tombstone observer remarked, "He was a bad gunman always but usually took care to keep himself on the safe side of the law, or to be in such a position to talk his way out of trouble. In this event, too, he thought that he had all things planned to escape the results of his misdeed, but he slipped."

On December 30 he was arraigned in District Court and pleaded not guilty. After various legal maneuverings, Frank, on the advice of his lawyers, changed his original pleading to guilty. A man named Harry Smith, who as a young boy in 1881 had come to Cochise County with his parents, later said that Frank was a man who killed for the thrill of it, a "genuine badman, treacherous and dangerous." Harry Smith's assessment of the infamous gunslinger was shared by the court. He was sentenced to life imprisonment at the Yuma Territorial Prison.

Sheriff Slaughter traveled with Frank to Yuma, arriving with several other new prisoners. The luster of gleaming pearl studs and silver firing devices had quickly dulled into prison convict No. 632, height five feet, seven inches, weight 135 pounds. Frank Leslie was allowed to keep his own boots because the prison guards could not find shoes small enough to fit him. He was also allowed to keep the mustache.

In the end, the slippery Leslie would again talk his way out, pardoned for good behavior and because of lingering questions about the quality of evidence that had convicted him in the first place. Interviewed several years later by a reporter from San Francisco, Leslie would reminisce about his life, how he had been misunderstood, and how the death of Mollie was not his doing. Letters and petitions for his release arrived at the Yuma penitentiary and, in 1896, his case was brought before Arizona's Territorial governor. Once again, Buckskin Frank walked.

On July 14, 1889, Mollie had been buried on the Magnolia ranch close to where she fell. A number of her friends from the Bird Cage made their way out to the ranch to say their good-byes. It was quiet in the Swisshelm Mountains. Meanwhile, back in Tombstone, the Bird Cage still rocked. "Mr. Bignon has a good company always on the boards," reported the *Epitaph*. "It is a pleasant place to go and spend a few hours of the evenings."

CHAPTER 16

Bird Cage Reveries

Tombstone was a boomtown. Boomtowns go bust. In May 1886, a fire destroyed the pumps of one of the main companies. Eventually, through the next few years, one by one, the clanking and thumping of the pump houses quieted, the hoisting works shut down, and the mule trains disappeared. The underground water became impossible to control, even with the use of the pumps. The land that had given up some of its treasures refused to give up any more. Only a handful of mines kept at it, along with a few determined souls still seeking fortune in the open diggings. Tombstone was gradually returning to a state of nature.

Despite the calamitous decline of Tombstone's principal industry, Joe Bignon tried everything he could to keep the Bird Cage going. He again remodeled the place, brought in some new acrobats and dancers, and even set up torchlight parades down Allen Street, a kind of last hurrah to arouse interest. But the vanishing population had spelled the end of the halcyon days of the Bird Cage. It could still attract soldiers and some ranchers and some of the miners who hung around, but the reduced numbers meant economic doom. Like Billy Hutchinson before him, Joe Bignon finally succumbed. He sold the building, closed its doors in the summer of 1892, and shipped the props to Albuquerque.

Bignon briefly returned to Tombstone and for a time ran variety performances at the Crystal Palace saloon, engaging a few of the Bird Cage old-timers such as singer Ella Ward and seriocomic Jessie Reed. He made a go of it for about two years, finally giving up again to return to New Mexico. When the town recovered, he said, he would return.

Later, when gold was discovered in Pearce, Arizona, Joe and Minnie were on the move again. After dabbling in real estate, Joe converted a saloon in Pearce into a moving picture theater. But it wasn't like the old days at the Bird Cage. The money just wasn't there.

Now the silver lode was gone, the mines full of water, the pumps submerged in the depths of the shafts and tunnels. The writer Owen Wister wrote to his mother that Tombstone "has a past but nothing else. . . . houses, saloons, hotels, large shops—their doors nailed up and the panes cracked out of the windows."

The swirl of miners, cowmen, stage drivers, prospectors, gamblers, and dance hall girls stilled. The Bird Cage was quiet. The boards of the Bird Cage stage emptied; the magicians, monologists, mimics, and musicians moved on.

On to Vaudeville

I shot an arrow into the air;
it fell to earth I know not where.
I lose more damn arrows that way.

—One of countless vaudeville jokes

Some of the entertainers who had braved the audiences at the smoky variety halls and rowdy honkytonks such as the Bird Cage would later join impresarios of nearly all kinds in a lusty new American invention called vaudeville. Variety stages such as the Bird Cage were vaudeville's cradles.

Like many forms of theater, dance, and music, vaudeville had its origins in Europe. In France, vaudeville referred to light pastoral plays with musical interludes. By the late eighteenth century, the Theatre de Vaudeville in Paris was a thriving attraction. In the United States vaudeville would come to mean something different, an amalgam of several kinds of entertainment.

Although minstrelsy, burlesque, and variety were the predominant forms of American popular entertainment after the Civil War, as early as 1871 the Great Vaudeville Company opened at Weisiger's Hall in Louisville, Kentucky. A typical vaudeville show offered the audience a little bit of everything in eight to fourteen acts, or *turns*. The average show had about ten turns and included magic segments, musical numbers (especially solo and duet vocals), dance numbers, combination song-and-dance acts, acrobatics, juggling, comic routines (monologists were popular), animal acts, celebrity cameos, and appearances by criminals, pugilists, and others in the news.

Its entertainment reflected life in America in the second half of the nineteenth century: immigration, fast-paced urban life, industrialization, temperance, women's suffrage, and social problems such as alcoholism. In 1883 a Boston circus and tent-show performer, Benjamin Franklin Keith, opened a "dime museum," a continuous form of live entertainment appealing to families. By March 1894 he opened his first B. F. Keith's Theater and, like the company in Louisville, called it vaudeville. Six- and eight-act shows ran continuously throughout the afternoon and evening, entertainment that was there for the public when they wanted it, at their convenience and not the theater's, the kind of hours the Bird Cage had offered to its own clientele for years.

Vaudeville impresario and entrepreneur Edward Albee, whose adopted son and namesake would later become a renowned playwright, once gave this view of vaudeville's popularity: "In vaudeville, there is always something for everybody, just as in every state and city, in every county and town in our democratic country, there is opportunity for everybody, a chance for all."

When the Bird Cage first opened, one of the notable performers was Mlle. De Granville, able to pick up large objects with her teeth. And now in vaudeville, it was Martha Farra, all 120 pounds of her, able, it was said, to hold up an automobile with twelve men in it while lying on her back on a board of nails. At the Bird Cage, it was *Uncle Tom's Cabin*, with a trained bloodhound on the trail of Eliza. In vaudeville, it was Beautiful Jim Key, a horse that could spell names, use the telephone, make change, and play the organ. The Bird Cage had the great wrestler Schumacher; vaudeville had Josefsson's Icelandic Troupe showing off the secret sports of Iceland, including wrestling with the feet. At the Bird Cage it was Joe Bignon in blackface; vaudeville had Al Jolson, who first tried his bellboy act in white face and later chalked on black on the advice of another performer on the bill. The rest, as they said in vaudeville, was history.

But if vaudeville kept the diversity and accessibility of the variety theaters, Keith and the other vaudeville innovators changed the atmosphere. They cleaned up the theaters, tamed the language, put most of the clothes back on the young women, and invited families to join the fun. Keith even hired female attendants specifically to work the street and the lobby to draw into the theater individuals who would not otherwise bring themselves or their children into variety halls. The Bird Cage Theatre had gambling, prostitution, and other assorted vices to whet the usual variety bill; Keith replaced them with short dramatic plays, silent movies, operettas and lectures. It wasn't the Bird Cage, but it was something for most everybody.

Keith opened one theater after another, some costing as much as a million dollars. His Boston theater alone catered to twenty-five thousand people a week. His continuous-performance system reportedly shuffled twelve thousand people through one theater on a single holiday. A chain of palatial theaters on the East Coast attracted performers and audiences to a more refined form of amusement—away from smoky bars and beer gardens into halls, some nearly magisterial. It was still madcap; it was still loud and boisterous; but it seemed safer.

A typical vaudeville bill seemed familiar to readers of the *Epitaph* or *Daily Nugget* who had seen ads placed by the Bird Cage. Arabian whirlwind tumblers teamed with jugglers, acrobats, aerialists, trick cyclists, hoofers, and comedians on the vaudeville stage. But they also teamed with

Inside the Bird Cage. (Courtesy of the Arizona State Historical Society.)

performers from the grand opera and renowned dramatists such as Sarah Bernhardt and Lillie Langtry.

For the Bird Cage, however, there was to be no vaudeville. After Joe Bignon, other owners tried to revive the Bird Cage but failed. It closed down in 1889.

Helldorado

At various times since 1889, the Bird Cage building has opened as a coffee shop and as a tourist attraction. It has remained relatively unchanged inside, more than a century after the frontier days. In 1929, the doors of the Bird Cage opened for the first Helldorado celebration, an event hosted by the remaining residents of Tombstone to honor the town's founding. The name of the event apparently had its origins in a miner's remark that appeared in the *Daily Nugget* in July 1881. The frustrated prospector told some relatives that many who came to Arizona seeking the legendary El Dorado had found, instead, a "Hell Dorado."

The title bewildered and somewhat annoyed the estimable John Clum, former operator of the *Epitaph,* returning to town and to a few of its survivors that he knew fifty years earlier. In a written account laced both with elements of fondness and sarcasm, Clum said the Helldorado literature "was equally lurid—and alluring," peddling the notion that the inhabitants of the boom years were engaged chiefly in "gambling, booze-guzzling and gunfighting; that the final arbiter of all disputes was the deadly six-shooter; that at least one dead man was provided for breakfast each morning; that . . . it was not uncommon for a man to bury his wife in the morning, kill a man before noon, and marry another woman before sundown."

For John Clum, the Bird Cage was the highlight of his return. On the first night, the room was quickly filled to capacity. At the invitation of Tombstone's mayor, Clum enjoyed seats in the royal box overlooking the footlights, "where I was able to indulge in a bit of wide-open flirtation with a fascinating flapper jig-dancer, much to her amusement—as well as that of the audience."

The Bird Cage was perhaps the single most popular attraction at the Helldorado. Annie Duncan, the Tombstone Nightingale, came back for the festivities, appearing on the stage with a voice weaker than in the '80s but with an enthusiasm undiminished. Her appearance brought an eruption of applause.

At the bar, aproned barkeeps stacked drinks on the dumbwaiter that rattled its load to the boxes above. Heavily rouged "commission girls" again plied their trade, except for the intimate encounters. The stage shook with dancers and jokesters and titillating humor. And in the dark recesses of the night, after some of the revelers had spent their energies and their money and retired to the street, others shoved aside the benches and cleared the floor. Just like forty years earlier, just as in the days of the hard-rock miners and cowboys, the days of the gamblers and the doves, the Bird Cage hosted a dance.

Paranormal Peculiarities

More than a hundred years after the Bird Cage Theatre's variety and gambling days, a woman and her young daughter visited Tombstone, where the girl had a frightening experience. Standing at the doorway of the Bird Cage, face ashen and voice trembling, the girl looked as if she had seen a ghost. "We were not in there alone, Mom," she stammered.

At first the mother treated the girl's claims with casual dismissiveness. But as the child persisted, the mother was later moved to investigate the question: Did otherworldly inhabitants still play in the box seats where ladies once entertained their paying customers; did comics and dancers still prance about on the decaying hardwood stage?

"Only after doing some research," she later wrote, "did I find out that Anna was not the first to become aware of such entities in what was, in its day, one of the wildest places in the west, with its saloon, casino, dance hall, prostitutes and theater."

Hundreds of visitors through the years have shared in the girl's experience, recounting the times they glimpsed images of folks wearing clothes from the 1800s and heard people singing and talking in the boxes. Some have claimed they smelled the faint odor of cigar smoke. Considering the number of cigars smoked at the Bird Cage Theatre in its heyday, that particular claim is, perhaps, not surprising. The alarm comes when several visitors report sightings of a ghostly man wearing a visor, walking across the stage. Some have even taken photographs and placed them on the World Wide Web, challenging others to disprove their claims.

The stories are legion. The owner of the Bird Cage, Bill Hunley—who purchased the establishment several decades ago—said that when he decided to put wooden statues of gunfighters in the theater as part of the tourist display, he had some uncommon problems with Wyatt Earp. The hat on the statue kept falling onto a poker table with no explainable cause. When he moved the Earp figure away from an area that the Clantons reportedly liked, the hat stayed on.

In claiming for the Bird Cage a prominent place in the paranormal, one Internet site has cooperated mightily. At "Bob and Shauna's Haunted Ghost Town Site," the Bird Cage ranks thirteenth in a list of the most haunted places in North America, just behind Alcatraz Island in San Francisco Bay.

And if the Bird Cage has ghosts, so do several other Tombstone historic sites. There's the street in front of the Aztec House Antique Shop, where an apparition of a woman in a long white dress has been seen wandering, even, it is said, blocking traffic on occasion. There's Big Nose Kate's Saloon, where ghosts of cowboys are sometimes observed standing in the doorways or sitting at the bar. There's Nellie Cashman's Restaurant, where paranormal beings sometimes move objects and make crashing noises. And, of course, there's Schieffelin Hall, where ghosts seem to be most active during town hall meetings. And there is a ghost that frequents an old bridge over the San Pedro River. Known as La Llorona, "the weeping woman," she searches the riverbanks for her children, whom, it is said, she drowned more than a hundred years ago.

Some individuals have even claimed personal relationships with the apparitions. One writer, believing herself attached paranormally with one of the Bird Cage dancers of the 1880s, produced a historical novel (more history than novel, she believes) that traces the dancer's life and even tries to correct certain historical assumptions made by researchers armed only with documentary evidence and not with insight gleaned from visions.

A Reunion

With or without the otherworldly, the Bird Cage is now a historical monument and a testament to the lives of the western boomtown. Some wild times occurred within its walls and outrageous characters passed through its doors.

But beyond the hijinks, tall tales, and nonstop frenetic pace, much that went on was warmly human. The story of Ed Wittig and his son is a good example.

At the head of the Bird Cage band most evenings stood the bewhiskered German violinist Ed Wittig. Born in Berlin in 1841, brought by his father to the United States prior to the Civil War, Wittig served in an Illinois regiment, then moved west in the late 1860s, playing the violin in show houses in Denver, Leadville, and other towns. He moved to Tombstone in 1881, leaving his family behind for a time. He had arranged for them to move to Tombstone, but communications became so irregular between Colorado and the fledging mining community that Wittig grew concerned.

Then one evening in 1882, a sixteen-year-old boy walked up to the box office at the Bird Cage and asked to see the orchestra leader. He was allowed in. As he walked through the crowd toward the stage, the acting troupe had reached a high point in its presentation. Violins played sweetly, and a climax neared. Suddenly the music stopped, and the actors suspended their performance. Ed Witting leaped from his chair and ran up the aisle to the boy, and all eyes fixed on the two of them. The boy was Ed Wittig's son.

Many years later, Ed Wittig Jr. remembered the warmth and camaraderie in the Bird Cage that night, how the cast and orchestra members and showgirls all shared in the reunion, how Billy Hutchinson passed out free tickets to the audience, and how, for several days thereafter, the Wittig family was the chief topic of conversation in Tombstone.

Honkytonk Memories

In the Bird Cage's netherworld of legend and fact, there are curious intersections. During Wyatt Earp's last years in California, he befriended a number of Hollywood actors who were beginning to portray the early West on the silver screen. The big events in Tombstone were now several decades past, and time and storytelling were beginning to redefine history and define legend.

Long ago, through most of the 1890s, the boards of the Bird Cage

William S. Hart in *The Bargain* (1914), his first full-length film. (Courtesy of the Library of Congress.)

stage rocked with the cancan and animal acts and wrestling matches, and with comedians, singers, and actors. And now, here was Wyatt Earp on a movie set in Hollywood with his friend William S. Hart, cowboy actor. And here was Charlie Chaplin, the great vaudevillian now moving on to motion pictures. It was on this movie set that Chaplin first met Wyatt Earp. He had heard of him. When introduced, Chaplin said, "You're the bloke from Arizona, aren't you? Tamed the baddies, huh?"

For one vibrant decade, the Bird Cage was the most famous honkytonk in America. Inside its walls, the frontier rollicked. In 1925, the *Star* looked back on those days and found inspiration:

> *Its founder dead*
> *Its players gone*
> *And audience scattered wide,*
> *The Bird Cage stands—*
> *A spectre!*

A Note on Sources

H istorical materials, including the diaries, reminiscences, and correspondence of pioneers, business records, photographs, and maps, are in the Tombstone Courthouse State Historic Park, the Arizona Historical Society, the Special Collections Department of the University of Arizona Library in Tucson, the San Pedro Valley Historical Society in Benson, Arizona, and the Bisbee Mining of Historical Museum in Bisbee, Arizona.

Many of the newspapers from the early days of Tombstone have survived. The University of Arizona and the Arizona Historical Society hold copies of the *Epitaph*, the *Daily Nugget*, and the *Independent*. The National Archives have much material from federal marshals and other law enforcement officers in Tombstone regarding outlaws, Native Americans, and other subjects.

The Arizona Department of Library, Archives, and Public Records in Phoenix has a collection of interviews obtained by writers who worked for the Works Progress Administration in the 1930s. These interviews provide extraordinary firsthand remembrances from ranchers, miners, and other average Americans working on the western frontier in the last decades of the nineteenth century. This department also holds a collection of Cochise County Justice of the Peace inquest reports that offer valuable nuggets of social history.

Endnotes

PROLOGUE

viii "Within her gilded cage confined": "The Contrast: The Parrot and the Wren," *The Complete Poetical Works of William Wordsworth* (London: Macmillan Co., 1888), reprinted by Columbia University, Academic Information Systems, Bartleby Library, at www.bartleby.com/145/ww711.html.

CHAPTER 1
A NAUGHTY ESTABLISHMENT

2 "Amost every man wore mustaches": Interview of Rosa Schuster, Arizona Writers Project, Arizona Department of Library, Archives, and Public Records.

2 "NOTICE! All Persons Entering This House": Tombstone Courthouse State Historic Park museum.

3 "Especially ingenious was the 'protector'": *The Gamblers* (Alexandria, Virginia: Time-Life Books, 1978), 146–7.

3 "Behind the bar was a luxurious painting": James Crane, "*Hold! The Story of the Attack on the Kinnear Stage,*" manuscript at University of Arizona Library, 6.

3 "In this artistic triumph": Richard Erdoes, *Saloons of the Old West* (New York: Knopf, 1979), 51.

4 "Comedian Eddie Foy, who had played": Eddie Foy and Alvin Harlow, *Clowning Through Life* (New York: E. P. Dutton & Company, 1928), 159.

4 "the last resort of the blasé": San Francisco *Call*, November 28, 1869.

4   "a moral penal colony": "Barbary MUSH-Cthulhu in 1890s San Francisco," available at website www.best.com/~gazissax/barbary.htm.

4   "Plain Talk and Beautiful Girls!": Jacqueline Baker Barnhart, *The Fair But Frail: Prostitution in San Francisco, 1849–1900* (Reno: University of Nevada Press, 1986), 32–3; Erdoes, 172.

5   "boxes that resembled 'so many pigeon holes'": Herbert Asbury, *The Barbary Coast: An Informal History of the San Francisco Underworld* (New York: Old Town Books, 1933), 128–9; David Dary, *Seeking Pleasure in the Old West* (New York: Alfred A. Knopf, 1995), 204; Samuel Dickson, *Tales of San Francisco* (Stanford, California: Stanford University Press, 1957), 40–41.

5   "Billy Hutchinson will guarantee satisfaction": *Tombstone Epitaph*, December 21, 1881.

5   "living pictures": *The Daily Nugget*, January 31, 1882.

6   "Shortly after midnight": Erdoes, 172.

6   "bucking the tiger": *Gamblers*, 87–8.

7   "the name of the Bird Cage": *Arizona Daily Star*, August 18, 1882.

8   "Prior to keeping those dates": *Arizona Daily Star*, February 10, 1929; Marshall Trimble, *In Old Arizona: True Tales of the Wild Frontier* (Phoenix: Golden West Publishers, 1993), 122.

8   "Workers from the Lucky Cuss": *Arizona Daily Star*, October 19, 1882.

9   "Lizette, the Flying Nymph": Robert C. Toll, *On With the Show: The First Century of Show Business in America* (New York: Oxford University Press, 1976), 68–9.

9   "A lady dressed in evening costume": Irving Zeidman, *The American Burlesque Show* (New York: Hawthorn Books, 1967), 29; American Memory Collection, "The American Variety Stage, Vaudeville and Popular Entertainment, 1870–1920," Library of Congress.

9   "Seated on wooden benches": Walter Noble Burns, *Tombstone: An Iliad of the Southwest* (Garden City, New York: Doubleday, Page & Company, 1927), 31.

11 "Successful performers were often rewarded": *Arizona Daily Star*, November 3, 1882; Pat Jahns, *The Frontier World of Doc Holliday* (New York: Hastings House Publishers, 1979), 220.

12 "took the chance": *Arizona Daily Star*, December 13, 1925.

12 "She's only a bird": "She's Only a Bird in a Gilded Cage," lyrics by Arthur Lamb, music by Harry Von Tilzer; Music Division, Harry Von Tilzer Collection, Library of Congress.

13 "Other versions of the story": "The Bird Cage Theatre Story," available at website www.tombstoneaz.net/birdcage.htm.

13 "There is also strong evidence": The Tunesmith's Database, website www.alright.com/home/mlp.

14 "After depositing two bits": *Arizona Daily Star,* October 19, 1882.

14 "At Bird Cage all of the time": Lynn Bailey, ed., *The Devil Has Foreclosed: The Private Journal of George Whitwell Parsons, Volume II, The Concluding Arizona Years, 1882–87* (Tucson: Westernlore Press, 1997), 40.

14 "The Bird Cage was the soul": *Missouri Republican,* February 5, 1888.

14 "Monday night last" and "As the ball advanced": *Arizona Daily Star,* October 22, 1882.

15 "First Appearance of Mr. Tommy Rosa": Text from Bird Cage handbill, Walter Noble Burns, 31–32.

15 "Long about two or three o'clock": *Arizona Daily Star,* February 10, 1929.

CHAPTER 2
ED SCHIEFFELIN FINDS SILVER IN GOOSE FLATS

17 "I can't say that": Dee Brown, *Wondrous Times on the Frontier* (Little Rock, Arkansas: August House Publishers, 1991), 262.

19 "The news of the fabulous Arizona strike": William Hattich, *Pioneer Magic* (New York: Vantage Press, 1964), 23.

19 "I came to Tombstone in '81": Interview of Charles Gordes, Arizona Writers Project, Arizona Department of Library, Archives, and Public Records.

20 "On the outskirts were tents": Quoted in Thomas H. Peterson, *The Tombstone Stagecoach Lines, 1878–1903: A Thesis Submitted to the Faculty of the Department of History.* Master of Arts, University of Arizona, Tucson, Arizona, 1968, 95.

20 "As is usually the case": *Arizona Daily Star,* August 23, 1879.

20 "Sustained by the grandeur": *The Daily Nugget,* December 31, 1881.

21 "Silence of the unpeopled hills": Neil Carmony, ed., *Apache Days and Tombstone Nights: John Clum's Autobiography, 1877–1887* (Silver City, New Mexico: High–Lonesome Books, 1997), 78.

21 "An army of prospectors" and "one of the greatest mining camps": *Report of the Acting Governor of Arizona Made to the Secretary of the Interior for the Year 1881* (Washington, D.C.: Government Printing Office, 1881), 18.

21 "O'Neill had recently performed as Jesus Christ": Dickson, 299.

21 "O'Neill purchased shares": *Tombstone Epitaph,* April 2, 1881, and *Arizona Daily Star,* March 31, 1881.

22 "Desperados, gunmen, officers": Interview of Charles Overlook, Arizona Writers Project, Arizona Department of Library, Archives, and Public Records.

23 "Over the years, of course": See account of recent statistical studies by Michael Bellesiles and Robert Dykstra in "Arms and the Man," *The Economist,* July 3, 1999.

24 "There are no cockroaches": Crane, 6–7; Suzann Ledbetter, *Nellie Cashman: Prospector and Trailblazer* (El Paso: Texas Western Press, 1993), 14–15.

24 "Most writers have the idea": Frank Waters, *The Earp Brothers of Tombstone* (Lincoln: University of Nebraska Press, 1976), 88.

24 "All sorts and conditions of men": Casey Tefertiller, *Wyatt Earp: The Life Behind the Legend* (New York: John Wiley & Sons, 1997), 107–108.

26 "I went to work in the mines": Interview of James Elmo Bartee, Arizona Writers Project, Arizona Department of Library, Archives, and Public Records.

27 "You could get out of life": Walter Zipf, "Ed Wittig: Pioneer Resident of Two Frontier Towns," *The Bisbee Daily Review,* September 23, 1934.

27 "Saloons, restaurants, hotels": W. Lane Rogers, ed., *When All Roads Led to Tombstone: A Memoir by John Pleasant Gray* (Boise, Idaho: Tamarack Books, 1998), 18.

CHAPTER 3
A DISTURBANCE IN TOMBSTONE

29 "That fight didn't take but about 30 seconds": John Stephens, ed., *Wyatt Earp Speaks* (Cambria Pines by the Sea, California: Fern Canyon Press, 1998), 294.

30 "There are some": Tefertiller, 40.

30 "road agents and other criminals": National Archives, RG 60, Records of the Department of Justice, Source–Chronological Files: Arizona, letters of Marshal Crowley P. Dake.

31 "The underlying cause": 47th Congress, 1st Session, Ex. Doc. No. 58, 2/2/1882.

32 "to pursue and bring to justice": Cooper to U.S. Secretary of State, 9/30/81, Arizona Writers Project, Arizona Department of Library, Archives, and Public Records.

34 "The Tombstone showdown": Jeff Sharlet, "Author's Methods Lead to Showdown Over Much-Admired Book on Old West," *The Chronicle of Higher Education,* June 11, 1999, A19–A20.

34 "Earpiana is actually": Glenn G. Boyer, *Wyatt Earp's Tombstone Vendetta* (Honolulu, Hawaii: Talei Publishers, 1993), 317.

CHAPTER 4
PLAYING THE DESERT

37 "Western emigration makes": *The Townsmen* (Alexandria, Virginia: Time–Life Books, 1975), 224.

38 "the 4–Paw's Monster Railroad Circus": *Tombstone Epitaph,* October 26, 1881.

38 "I have seen the elephant": A. C. Greene, "In 1800s, 'seeing an elephant' was quite an experience," *The Dallas Morning News,* June 6, 1999.

39 "Westerners named mines": Jennifer Lee Carrell, "How the Bard Won the West," *Smithsonian,* August 1998, 99–107.

39 "Shakespeare buffs": *The Townsmen,* 179–81; Ibid, 102–6.

39 "The choice of Hamlet": George R. MacMinn, *The Theater of the Golden Era in California* (Caldwell, Idaho: The Caxton Printers, 1941), 164.

41 "Across the west": Robert C. Allen, *Horrible Prettiness: Burlesque and the American Culture* (Chapel Hill: The University of North Carolina Press, 1991), 178.

41 "songwriter Daniel Decatur Emmett": Website www.musicals.com; "The Minstrel Show," Center for American Music, available at website www.pitt.edu/~amerimus/minstrel.htm

42 "Why is the letter T": Available at website www.talkinbroadway.com.

43 "When Harriet Beecher Stowe": "Minstrel Music in America: 1829–1865," available at website www.geocities.com/nashville/1856/origins.html.

44 "other little hot house plants": American Memory Collection, "Variety Stage English Plays," Library of Congress.

44 *"The Bohemian G–Yurl":* American Memory Collection, "The American Variety Stage, Vaudeville and Popular Entertainment, 1870–1920," Library of Congress.

44 "It sets out with respecting nothing": Allen, 136.

46 "Eight to one on the colors": Foy and Harlow, 107.

46 "Matt Morgan's statuary": Joe Laurie, *Vaudeville: From the Honky–Tonks to the Palace* (New York: Henry Holt and Company, 1953), 37.

46 "She is the most undressed actress" and "Shape artist": *The Townsmen,* 180–1; Toll, 208–9.

48 "They go crazy over a woman": Quoted in Toll, 221–2.

48 "The typical fare": *El Paso Times,* December 17, 1887.

48 "A newspaper in El Paso": Laurie, 11–12.

48 "Here screened from observation": *Arizona Daily Star,* June 22, 1884.

49 "They were essentially pubs": Website www.musicals101.com.

49 "I took her out one night": Ibid.

49 "music by the band": Quoted in Zeidman, 28.

50 "There were hurdy–gurdies": Quoted from *Idaho Statesman*, October 5, 1867, in Harold Briggs, "Early Variety Theatres in the Trans–Mississippi West," *Mid–America: An Historical Review*, July 1952, 195.

50 "Grotesque Dancing": John Myers Myers, *The Last Chance: Tombstone's Early Years* (Lincoln: University of Nebraska Press, 1995), 54.

50 "something similar to the Tivoli": *Arizona Daily Star*, September 27, 1882.

51 "The trapezes through which": Zeidman, 29; Erdoes, 177.

CHAPTER 5

BOOMING CULTURE IN THE BOOMTOWN

53 "The only attractive places": *San Diego Union*, July 14, 1880.

53 "Ordinarily, the bare association": *Tucson Weekly Citizen*, April 3, 1880.

54 "The town is not altogether lost": *Arizona Daily Star*, February 29, 1880.

54 "the musical society 'once put on an opera'": Interview of Charles Alton Overlook, Arizona Writers Project, Arizona Department of Library, Archives, and Public Records.

54 "John Clum, Indian agent": Carmony, 39.

56 "When any one of the proposed company": *The Daily Nugget*, January 7, 1882; Bailey, 41.

56 "*Andy Blake, or The Irish Diamond*": Odie B. Faulk, *Tombstone: Myth and Reality* (New York: Oxford University Press, 1972), 120–21.

56 "Shakespeare's ghost is prowling": *Arizona Daily Star*, February 23, 1880.

56 "with many new adobe buildings": *Arizona Daily Star*, March 31, 1879.

57 "Now landsmen all": Website www.musicals101.com.

58 "The production was called *Pinafore on Wheels*": Francois Cellier, *Gilbert and Sullivan and Their Operas* (New York: Little, Brown and Company, 1914), available at website http://diamond.idbsu.edu/gas/pinafore.

58 "Going by the name of May Bell": *Arizona Daily Star*, December 2, 1879.

60 "From Santa Barbara to San Bernardino": Glenn G. Boyer, ed., *I Married Wyatt Earp: The Recollections of Josephine Sarah Marcus Earp* (Tucson: The University of Arizona Press, 1976), 10–12.

60 "Joe Bignon opened the Theatre Comique": Pat Ryan, *Tombstone Theatre Tonight: A Chronicle of Entertainment on the Southwestern Mining Frontier* (Tucson: The Tucson Corral of the Westerners, 1966; part of the series "The Smoke Signal," No. 13, Spring 1966), 52.

61 "Ethiopian Specialities": Rosemary Gipson, *The History of Tucson Theatre Before 1906: An M.A. Thesis Submitted to the Faculty of the Department of Drama*. Master of Arts, University of Arizona, Tucson, Arizona, 1967.

61 "Booth's Theatre production of *Flying Scud*": Myers, 52–3; Faulk, 119; Ryan, 53.

61 "After an appearance by Miss Jeffrey–Lewis": *Tombstone Epitaph*, November 30, 1880.

62 "Meet Pearl Ardine": *The Townsmen*, 173.

62 "professional actor Robert McWade": *Tombstone Epitaph*, April 16, 1881.

63 "It is now a pile of dry mud": *Tombstone Epitaph*, April 28, 1881.

63 "It was not gaudy or decorative": Faulk, 115–6.

63 "W. A. Cuddy, an experienced actor": *The Daily Nugget*, September 16, 1881; Claire E. Willson, "Pioneer Playhouse of Tombstone," *Arizona Highways*, October 1939, 14; Brown, 41.

64 "The amateur talent of Tombstone": John W. Parsons diary, excerpted in *The Tombstone Maverick*, May 14, 1998; Carmony, 39.

64 "Back in San Francisco": Willson, "Pioneer Playhouse of Tombstone," 15.

65 "The play that evening was Macbeth": Typescript of reading in Clum scrapbook, Special Collections, University of Arizona Library, quoted in Ryan, 64.

CHAPTER 6
THE HONKYTONK OF ALLEN STREET

67 "As good as San Francisco": *Arizona Daily Star*, February 17, 1929.

68 "Sixth Street Opera House": *Arizona Daily Star*, February 10, 1929.

68 "Billy was in San Francisco": *Tombstone Epitaph*, December 19, 1881.

68 "Madame DuPree, a 'renowned pedestrienne'": *Tombstone Epitaph*, December 26, 1881.

68 "But at 517 Allen Street": *Tombstone Epitaph*, December 26, 1881.

69 "Miss Irene Baker ingratiated herself": *Tombstone Epitaph*, December 22, 1881.

69 "Billy spiced the place": Receipts, Bird Cage Theatre Museum.

70 "at the Bird Cage was Mlle. De Granville": *The Townsmen*, 173.

70 "comic duo of Burns and Trayers": *The Daily Nugget*, December 23, 1881.

71 "It shared certain characteristics": Brown, 199.

71 "We were not particular": *Arizona Daily Star*, December 13, 1925.

71 "person can spend several hours": *Arizona Daily Star*, November 23, 1882.

71 "The pink of perfection": *The Daily Nugget*, February 4, 1882.

72 "As new specialties": *The Daily Nugget*, February 17, 1882.

72 "You could sleep in the midst": Rogers, 21.

72 "Tombstone was never": Interview of Rosa Schuster, Arizona Writers Project, Arizona Department of Library, Archives, and Public Records.

74 "It was a great resort": William Breakenridge, *Helldorado: Bringing the Law to the Mesquite* (Lincoln: University of Nebraska Press, 1992), 261–2.

74 "When the Hutchinsons first opened": Ben T. Traywick, "Tombstone's Bird Cage," in *Best of the Wild West* (Harrisburg, Pennsylvania: Cowles Publishers, 1996), 247.

74 "I was very green": Ryan, 69–70.

CHAPTER 7
THE SOILED DOVES

77 "Ghastly picture": John Myers Myers, *Tombstone's Early Years* (Lincoln: University of Nebraska Press, 1995), 70.

77 "Some theaters featured": Barnhart, 74–5.

78 "It was a wild place": Interview of Mrs. Jacob Scheerer, Arizona Writers Project, Arizona Department of Library, Archives, and Public Records.

78 "Tombstone city council voted": *Tombstone Daily Record–Epitaph*, September 18, 1885; Anne M. Butler, *Daughters of Joy, Sisters of Misery: Prostitutes in the American West, 1865–90.* (Urbana, Illinois: University of Illinois Press, 1985), 76–79.

78 "A fallen angel was arrested": Douglas Martin, *Tombstone's Epitaph* (Norman: University of Oklahoma Press, 1997), 27–28.

79 "The women of the camp's 'nether world'": Interview of Edward Wittig Jr., Arizona Writers Project, Arizona Department of Library, Archives, and Public Records.

79 "Madame Moustache": Ben T. Traywick, *Eleanor Dumont, Alias Madam Moustache* (Tombstone: Red Marie's Bookstore, 1990), 8.

79 "Elderly gentlemen would do well": Paula Mitchell Marks, *And Die in the West: The Story of the O.K. Corral Gunfight* (Norman: University of Oklahoma Press, 1989), 49.

80 "Helen Lind and her husband": Biographical sketch of Helen Yonge Lind, Arizona Historical Society.

80 "To be sure, there are frequent dances": Bailey, *Tombstone From a Woman's Point of View*, 22.

81 "Them women always looked down": Ben T. Traywick, *Hell's Belles of Tombstone* (Tombstone: Red Marie's Bookstore, 1993), 18.

81 "The mortality amongst these girls": Interview of Charles Gordes, Arizona Writers Project, Arizona Department of Library, Archives, and Public Records.

81 "All I know, I have been living with her": Cochise County Coroner's Inquests, August 17, 1888, Arizona Department of Library, Archives, and Public Records.

82 "kept out of Pascual Negro's": Charles L. Sonnichsen, *Billy King's Tombstone: The Private Life of an Arizona Boom Town* (Caldwell, Idaho: The Caxton Printers, 1942), 98–9.

82 "remembered Samantha as 'Mrs. Fallon'": Stephens, 171–2.

82 "Magarita strutted around the table": Cy Martin, *Whiskey and Wild Women: An Amusing Account of the Saloons and Bawds of the Old West* (New York: Hart Publishing Company, 1974), 26; Traywick, "Tombstone's Bird Cage," 248–9.

83 "The wages of sin": Traywick, "Tombstone's Bird Cage," 250–1.

CHAPTER 8
THE MYSTERY OF SADIE EARP

86 "My blood demanded excitement": Boyer, *I Married Wyatt Earp*, 7.

86 "The bewitched but duplicitous Johnny": Harriet and Fred Rochlin, *Pioneer Jews* (Boston: Houghton Mifflin, 1984), 203.

86 "Bat Masterson, and a score of old–timers": Bob Boze Bell, *The Illustrated Life and Times of Doc Holliday* (Phoenix: Tri–Star–Boze Publications, 1995), 36; Stephens, 27.

87 "told him in the presence of a crowd": Bell, 36.

87 "standing within ten feet": *Tombstone Epitaph*, March 20, 1882.

88 "In a few brief moments": Ibid.

88 "Morgan Earp's assassination": *Tombstone Epitaph*, March 27 and 30, 1882.

88 "Each of the horsemen were armed": *Sacramento Daily Record–Union*, January 15, 1882.

91 "even her name is now a matter of debate": Tony Ortega, "Who Is This?," *Phoenix New Times*, December 24, 1998.

92 "Everything about it": Ibid.

92 "If it isn't Josie": Glenn G. Boyer, *Wyatt Earp: Facts, Volume Two: Childhood and Youth of Wyatt's Wife, Josephine Sarah Marcus* (Rodeo, New Mexico: Historical Research Associates, 1996), 6.

CHAPTER 9
TALL TALES AND SOMEWHAT TRUE

94 "Luridly, feverishly": Corio, 34.

94 "She was a radiant performer": "Lotta Crabtree: fairy star of the gold rush," in Nevada County Gold Online at website www.ncgold.com.

94 "Ed Wittig Jr., son of the Bird Cage": Zipf, *The Bisbee Daily Review,* September 23, 1934.

95 "Lotta's brother, Jack Crabtree": Willson, 21–2.

95 "Awful. Rats. Take her out": Marks, 167; Burns, 150–1; Traywick, "Tombstone's Bird Cage," 249.

96 "Those girls had to go": *Arizona Daily Star,* February 17, 1929.

96 "experience of the English Opera Company": *Arizona Daily Star,* December 9, 1879.

97–98 "Sure, Johnny, I'm your huckleberry": "The Bird Cage Theatre Story," available at website www.tombstoneaz.net/birdcage.htm.

98–99 "A difficulty occurred yesterday": Tefertiller, 183; *Tucson Weekly Citizen,* January 22, 1882.

99 "I'll tell you who the Lord loves best": Edward Jervey, "Methodism in Arizona: The First Seventy Years," *Arizona and the West,* Winter 1961, 348.

101 "the one Curly Bill made dance": Lynn Bailey, *A Tenderfoot in Tombstone: The Private Journal of George Westwell Parsons, The Turbulent Years, 1880–82* (Tucson: Westernlore Press, 1996), 146.

102 "a bunch of hair": Traywick, "Tombstone's Bird Cage," 249.

102 "*The Cake Walk*": Toll, 155.

103 "Eliza's Escape on the Floating Ice": Tom Show Flyers—Downies Spectacular Company; handbills from the Harry Birdoff Collection, Harriet Beecher Stowe Center, Hartford, Connecticut, materials available at website www.iath.virginia.edu/utc/onstage/bills2/tsflyer21.html.

103 "After something of a fight": *Arizona Daily Star,* May 8, 1930.

CHAPTER 10
WRESTLIN' AND HOOFIN', DANCIN' AND SINGIN'

105 "Ethiopian acting": *Arizona Daily Star,* November 14, 1882.

105 "grotesque Dancing, Leg Mania": *The Daily Nugget,* February 17, 1882.

107 "Comedian Eddie Foy had played": American Memory Collection, "The American Variety Stage: Vaudeville and Popular Entertainment, 1870–1920," Library of Congress.

107 "I was determined to be nonchalant": *The Townsmen*, 174–6.

107 "Bat Masterson was just in the act": "The Eddie Foy Incident," at website www./geocities.com/athens/troy/9894/eddiefoy.htm.

107 "He had just purchased an eleven–dollar suit": Tefertiller, 24.

107 "Our engagement was at a concert hall": Foy and Harlow, 159.

109 "J. P. 'lavished money on her'": *The Townsmen*, 195; Traywick, "Tombstone's Bird Cage," 251; *Tombstone Republican*, September 15, 1883.

110 "Wells was reported drowned": Leo Banks, "Billy Hutchinson's Ribald Bird Cage Theatre," *Arizona Highways*, September 1996, 21.

110 "Wrestling match to a fine house": Bailey, *The Devil Has Foreclosed*, 100.

110 "A ponderous bar of iron": *Tombstone Epitaph*, January 3, 1886.

111 "The money is up": *Daily Tombstone*, May 3, 1886; Traywick, "Tombstone's BirdCage," 254.

112 "I am willing to fight": Michael Isenburg, *John L. Sullivan and His America* (Urbana: University of Illinois Press, 1994), 117.

112 "I believe no man": *National Police Gazette*, April 5, 1884.

114 "I never saw him": Interview of James Wolf, Arizona Writers Project, Arizona Department of Library, Archives, and Public Records.

114 "Of course the hostesses": Ibid.

115 "Druggist John Yonge": Biographical sketch of Helen Yonge Lind, Arizona Historical Society.

115 "You are not as big a man": *Arizona Weekly Citizen*, March 29, 1884; *National Police Gazette*, April 19, 1884.

115 "Jake Kilrain in the blazing sun": Isenberg, 315–23; Laurie, 120.

116 "We had old John L. Sullivan": Interview of Erma Hayes, November 10, 1938, American Memory Collection, Library of Congress.

CHAPTER 11
GAMBLING MANIA

117 "The profession of gamblers": *Arizona Weekly Star*, March 3, 1881, and August, 16, 1883.

118 "Cockfight Tonight": William Kelly, *Gamblers of the Old West: Gambling Men and Women of the 1880s* (Las Vegas: B & F Enterprises, 1995), 161.

118 "The belligerent portion of the community": A. C. Greene, "In 1800s, 'seeing an elephant' was quite an experience," *The Dallas Morning News*, June 6, 1999.

119 "at the Keno game": *Tombstone Epitaph*, September 24, 1880.

119 "a device called a casekeeper": John R. Sanders, "Faro: Favorite Gambling Game of the Frontier," *Wild West*, October 1996, Vol. 9, 62.

119 "complicated by combination betting": "Monte and Faro, the Miners' Favorite Games," available at website http://home.pacbell.net/elpayne/faro.html. "Luke Short and Charlie Storms": Sanders, 62.

120 "The games were as crooked": Interview of Charles Gordes, Arizona Writers Project, Arizona Department of Library, Archives, and Public Records.

121 "the great high-roller gamblers": Kelly, 152.

121 "Some of those who participate": Lynn R. Bailey, ed., *Tombstone from a Woman's Point of View: The Correspondence of Clara Spalding Brown, July 7, 1880, to November 14, 1882* (Tucson, Arizona: Westernlore Press, 1998), 89.

121 "special poker game at the Bird Cage": Willson, 13–14.

CHAPTER 12
THE CLIENTELE

123 "the soul of Tombstone": *Tombstone Epitaph*, April 29, 1884.

123 "I was only a prospector": Interview of Charles Gordes, Arizona Writers Project, Arizona Department of Library, Archives, and Public Records.

124 "More difficult than I imagined": Bailey, *A Tenderfoot in Tombstone*, diary entry of March 18, 1880, 31.

125 "One of the miners, Thomas Stevenson": Inquest of James Tully, November 13, 1882, Cochise County Coroner's Inquests, Arizona Department of Library, Archives, and Public Records.

125 "All dressed in simple, plain clothes": Interview of Ed Wittig Jr., Arizona Writers Project, Arizona Department of Library, Archives, and Public Records.

126 "for the sake of a new face": Faulk, 111.

127 "Fort Huachuca was home": "Fort Huachuca, AZ," U.S. Army Intelligence Center and Fort Huachuca, Public Affairs Office, Fort Huachuca, 1999, 1.

127 "What money the soldiers did not throw": Interview of Charles Gordes, Arizona Writers Project, Arizona Department of Library, Archives, and Public Records.

128 "We take a man here": Bell, 46.

129 "His dress consists of a flannel shirt": Joseph Rosa, *The Gunfighter: Man or Myth?* (Norman: University of Oklahoma Press, 1969), 70–71.

129   "They may have harbored": Rogers, 12.

CHAPTER 13
"THE CHINESE MUST GO"

131   "yellow-skinned, pig-tailed": Interview of Kathlyn Lathrop, Arizona Writers Project, Arizona Department of Library, Archives, and Public Records.

132   "Chinese laborers in Arizona Territory": Lawrence Fong, "Sojourners and Settlers: The Chinese Experience in Arizona," *The Journal of Arizona History*, Autumn, 1980.

132   "an ignorant, filthy": "The Promise of Gold: Tucson's Chinese Heritage: Building the Southern Pacific Railroad," available at website http://dizzy.library. arizona.edu/images/chamet/railroad.html.

133   "The Chinese worked as launderers": Ben T. Traywick, *The Chinese Dragon in Tombstone* (Tombstone: Red Marie's Bookstore, 1989), 1–7.

133   "led to China Mary": Eddie Foronda, "Tombstone's Other History," available at web site www.netgallery.com/~eforondo/tombstn.htm.

135   "A committee of ten": *Tombstone Epitaph*, July 25, 1880, and July 1, 1882.

135   "disposed to defend their rights": Bailey, Lynn R., ed., *Tombstone from a Woman's Point of View*, 20.

136   "in the neighborhood of Crittenden": *Tombstone Epitaph*, April 24, 1882.

136   "The Chinese are the least desired": Eric Clements, "Bust and Bust in the Mining West," *Journal of the West*, October 1996, 45–6; *The Miners* (Alexandria, Virginia: Time–Life Books, 1976), 109.

136   "To expect a business man": *Tombstone Epitaph*, May 7, 1886.

137   "For some reason...the burro preferred remaining": *Daily Tombstone*, March 9, 1886.

137   "Colonel Herring": *Tombstone Epitaph*, May 5, 1886.

138   "The nativist impulse": Clements, 46.

138   "A photographer gathered them together": Joe Cummings, "Sweet & Sour Times on the Border: A Review of Chinese Immigration to Mexico," available at website www.mexconnect.com/mex_/travel/jcummings/jcchina.html.

CHAPTER 14
THE JOE AND MINNIE SHOW

139   "Joe Bignon had yearned": Willson, 23–4.

140   "'Ethiopian acting' skits": *Arizona Daily Star*, December 14, 1882.

140   "Joe stayed in character": Banks, 21.

140   "San Francisco's Theatre Comique": Gipson, 79.

141   "Six-feet tall and 230 pounds": Sonnichsen, 108–9; *Tombstone Epitaph*, May 18, 1889.

142   "Wonder of Wonders": *Tombstone Prospector*, April 13, 1887.

142   "Tyrolian warbling": *Tombstone Prospector*, October 22, 1887.

144   "Charley looked at the man": *Tombstone Prospector*, May 11, 1889; Sonnichsen, 109; *Tombstone Epitaph*, May 12, 1889.

144   "A little episode not down on the bills": Douglas Martin, *Tombstone's Epitaph*, 25.

145   "Of a moral tone": *Tombstone Prospector*, April 10, 1889.

CHAPTER 15
THE TRAGEDY OF BIRD CAGE MOLLIE AND BUCKSKIN FRANK

147   "smooth-talking, blue-eyed Leslie": *The Daily Nugget,* June 10, 1880; Don Chaput, *"Buckskin Frank" Leslie* (Tucson: Westernlore Press, 1999), 11–18.

147   "the Oriental Saloon, as elegant": *Tombstone Epitaph*, July 22, 1889.

148   "When sober he is gentlemanly": *Tombstone Epitaph*, July 12, 1889.

148   "a silver slotted plate": Sonnichsen, 26; "Family, Friends and Foes of Wyatt Earp," quote on website www.dacc.cc.il.us/~mcoleman/wyatt4.html.

148   "amorous advances toward May Killeen": *Tombstone Epitaph*, August 25, 1880.

148   "The causes which led": *Tombstone Epitaph*, June 26, 1880.

149   "You paper men": *San Francisco Chronicle*, October 3, 1881.

149   "Billy did not distinguish himself": *Tombstone Epitaph*, October 23, 1881.

150   "Leslie went out the back way": Interview of Ed Wittig Jr., Arizona Writers Project, Arizona Department of Library, Archives, and Public Records; Myers, 238.

152   "Stand perfectly still, my dear": Douglas Martin, *Silver, Sex and Six Guns: Tombstone Saga of the Life of Buckskin Frank Leslie* (Tombstone: Tombstone Epitaph, 1962), 17–22; Colin Rickards, *"Buckskin Frank" Leslie: Gunman of Tombstone* (El Paso: Texas Western College Press, 1964), 6–10; Burns, 162; Chaput, 82.

152   "chasing Geronimo's Apaches": Record Group 92, Records of the Quartermaster General, Persons and Articles Hired, June 1883, National Archives and Records Administration, Washington, D.C.

152   "He had a fine voice": Quoted in Ben T. Traywick, *The Chronicles of Tombstone* (Tombstone: Red Marie's Bookstore, 1994), 161.

152 "He was quite an agreeable man": Interview of Betty Spicer, Arizona Writers Project, Arizona Department of Library, Archives, and Public Records.

153 "Take in yer leg": *Tombstone Epitaph*, December 9, 1926; *Arizona Daily Star*, February 10, 1929.

153 "I walked up to the corner": Mollie Williams testimony at the Inquest of W. J. Mason, May 19, 1884, Justice of the Peace Inquests, Arizona Department of Library, Archives, and Public Records; Sonnichsen, 33.

154 "everybody was making fun of it": Stephens, 176.

154 "I'll knock down the first son of a bitch": *Tombstone Epitaph*, July 26, 1880.

154 "In the back room of Corrigan's Saloon": Ibid.

155 "Piano player Ollie Callister": Rickards, 26.

155 "in the Swisshelm Mountains": Traywick, *Hell's Belles of Tombstone*, 29.

156 "A drunken Leslie found James Neil": Interview of James Neil, July 14, 1889, Coroner's Inquest, Mollie Edwards, Arizona Department of Library, Archives, and Public Records.

156 "he was bound to follow him": Interview of LeRoy Moody, Mollie Edwards Justice of the Peace Inquest, July 12, 1889, Arizona Department of Library, Archives, and Public Records.

156 "he was in a bad hole": Rogers, 38.

156 "He was a bad gunman": Interview of Betty Spicer, Arizona Writers Project, Arizona Department of Library, Archives, and Public Records.

157 "a genuine badman, treacherous and dangerous": Interview of Harry Smith, Arizona Writers Project, Arizona Department of Library, Archives, and Public Records.

157 "Sheriff Slaughter traveled with Frank": Carl Breihan and Wayne Montgomery, *Forty Years on the Wild Frontier* (Greenwich, Connecticut: Devin–Adair Publishers, 1985), 124.

157 "Once again, Buckskin Frank walked": Cochise County Minute Books, Cochise County Courthouse, Bisbee, Arizona; Breihan and Montgomery, 124.

157 "Mr. Bignon has a pleasant place to go": Douglas Martin, *Silver, Sex and Six Guns*, 49–51; *Tombstone Epitaph*, July 24, 1889.

CHAPTER 16
BIRD CAGE REVERIES

159 "Boomtowns go bust": Clements, 41–2.

160 "when gold was discovered in Pearce, Arizona": *Tombstone Epitaph*, July 19, 1890; *The Bisbee Review*, December 8, 1925.

160 "Tombstone 'has a past but nothing else'": Fanny Wister, ed., *Owen Wister Out West: His Journals and Letters* (Chicago: University of Chicago Press, 1958), 209.

160 "I shot an arrow into the air": "June Carr Vaudeville routines," available at website www.jtr.com/junecarr/jokes.htm.

161 "In vaudeville, there is always something for everybody": American Memory Collection, "The American Variety Stage: Vaudeville and Popular Entertainment, 1870–1920," Library of Congress.

162 "In vaudeville, it was Beautiful Jim Key": Laurie, 33, 165, and 129.

162 "A typical vaudeville bill": Interview of Alfred O. Philipp, Arizona Writers Project, Arizona Department of Library, Archives, and Public Records.

164 "seeking the legendary El Dorado": Tefertiller, 169.

164 "the Helldorado literature 'was equally lurid'": *Helldorado, 1879–1929: The Semi-Centennial Celebration of the Founding of the Famous Mining Camp of Tombstone, Arizona* (Tombstone: Tombstone Epitaph, 1999), 4.

164 "where I was able to indulge": *Phoenix Republican*, October 26, 1939.

164 "the Bird Cage hosted a dance": *Helldorado*, 9.

165 "We were not in there alone": Sandy Shaw, "Ghosts, Phantoms and Apparitions of Our Haunted Deserts," *Desert/USA*, October 1998, available at website www.desertusa.com/mag98/oct/stories/hdesert.html.

165 "wooden statues of gunfighters": Ted Wood, *Ghosts of the Southwest: The Phantom Gunslinger and Other Real-Life Hauntings* (New York: Walker and Company, 1997), 21.

166 "Bob and Shauna's Haunted Ghost Town Site": Accessible at website www.inconnect.com/ghostown/haunts.htm.

166 "the Aztec House Antique Shop": Wood, 7.

167 "Ed Wittig leaped from his chair": Interview of Ed Wittig Jr., Arizona Writers Project, Arizona Department of Library, Archives, and Public Records; Zipf, *The Bisbee Daily Review*, September 23, 1934.

168 "You're the bloke": Quote accessible at website www.techline.com/~nicks/birth.htm.

168 "Its founder dead": J. F. Weadock, "Only Shadows of Bygone Days Haunt Birdcage," *Arizona Daily Star*, December 13, 1925.

Bibliography

Allen, Robert C. *Horrible Prettiness: Burlesque and the American Culture*. Chapel Hill: The University of North Carolina Press, 1991.

Asbury, Herbert. *The Barbary Coast: An Informal History of the San Francisco Underworld*. New York: Old Town Books, 1933.

Bailey, Lynn R., ed. *Tombstone from a Woman's Point of View: The Correspondence of Clara Spalding Brown, July 7, 1880, to November 14, 1882*. Tucson: Westernlore Press, 1998.

———. *The Devil Has Foreclosed: The Private Journal of George Whitwell Parsons, Volume II, The Concluding Arizona Years, 1882–87*. Tucson: Westernlore Press, 1997.

———. *A Tenderfoot in Tombstone: The Private Journal of George Whitwell Parsons: The Turbulent Years, 1880–82*. Tucson: Westernlore Press, 1996.

Bakarich, Sarah. *Gunsmoke: The True Story of Old Tombstone*. Sierra Vista, Arizona: Gateway Publishing Company, 1962.

Banks, Leo, "Billy Hutchinson's Ribald Bird Cage Theatre," *Arizona Highways* (September 1996).

Barnhart, Jacqueline Baker. *The Fair But Frail: Prostitution in San Francisco, 1849–1900*. Reno: University of Nevada Press, 1986.

Barra, Allen. *Inventing Wyatt Earp: His Life and Many Legends*. New York: Carroll & Graf, 1999.

Bell, Bob Boze. *The Illustrated Life and Times of Doc Holliday*. Phoenix: Tri-Star-Boze Publications, 1995.

Boyer, Glenn G. *Wyatt Earp: Facts, Volume Two: Childhood and Youth of Wyatt's Wife, Josephine Sarah Marcus*. Rodeo, New Mexico: Historical Research Associates, 1996.

———. *Wyatt Earp's Tombstone Vendetta*. Honolulu, Hawaii: Talei Publishers, 1993.

Boyer, Glenn G., ed. *I Married Wyatt Earp (The Recollections of Josephine Sarah Marcus Earp)*. Tucson: The University of Arizona Press, 1976.

Bradley, Ian, "Changing the Tune: Popular Music in the 1890s," *History Today* (July 1992).

Breakenridge, William. *Helldorado: Bringing the Law to the Mesquite*. Lincoln: University of Nebraska Press, 1992.

Breihan, Carl, and Wayne Montgomery. *Forty Years on the Wild Frontier*. Greenwich, Connecticut: Devin-Adair Publishers, 1985.

Brent, Lynton. *The Bird Cage: A Theatrical Novel of Early Tombstone*. Philadelphia: Dorrance & Company, 1945.

Briggs, Harold, "Early Variety Theaters in the Trans-Mississippi West," *Mid-America: An Historical Review* (July 1952).

Brown, Dee. *Wonderous Times on the Frontier*. Little Rock: August House Publishers, 1991.

Brown, Robert L. *Saloons of the American West: An Illustrated Chronicle*. Denver: Sundance Books, 1978.

Burns, Walter Noble. *Tombstone: An Iliad of the Southwest*. Garden City, New York: Doubleday, Page & Company, 1927.

Butler, Anne M. *Daughters of Joy, Sisters of Misery: Prostitutes in the American West, 1865–90*. Urbana: University of Illinois Press, 1985.

Calhoun, Frederick S. *The Lawmen: United States Marshals and Their Deputies, 1789–1989*. New York: Penguin Books, 1991.

Canty, J. Michael, ed. *History of Mining in Arizona*. Tucson: Mining Club of the Southwest Foundation, 1987.

Carmony, Neil, ed. *Apache Days and Tombstone Nights: John Clum's Autobiography, 1877–1887*. Silver City, New Mexico: High-Lonesome Books, 1997.

Carrell, Jennifer Lee, "How the Bard Won the West," *Smithsonian* (August 1998).

Cellier, Francois. *Gilbert and Sullivan and Their Operas*. New York: Little, Brown and Company, 1914.

Chaput, Don. *"Buckskin Frank" Leslie*. Tucson: Westernlore Press, 1999.

Clements, Eric, "Bust and Bust in the Mining West," *Journal of the West* (October 1996).

Corio, Ann. *This Was Burlesque*. New York: Grosset and Dunlap, 1968.

Crane, James. *Hold! The Story of the Attack on the Kinnear Stage*. Manuscript at University of Arizona Library.

Dary, David. *Seeking Pleasure in the Old West*. New York: Alfred A. Knopf, 1995.

Dickson, Samuel. *Tales of San Francisco*. Stanford, California: Stanford University Press, 1957.

Elliott, Robert S., "Tombstone's Bird Cage Theatre Unveils Poker Room," *Inside Tucson Business* (February 26, 1996).

Erdoes, Richard. *Saloons of the Old West*. New York: Knopf, 1979.

Faulk, Odie B. *Arizona: A Short History*. Norman: University of Oklahoma Press, 1970.

———. *Tombstone: Myth and Reality*. New York: Oxford University Press, 1972.

Fong, Lawrence, "Sojourners and Settlers: The Chinese Experience in Arizona," *The Journal of Arizona History* (Autumn 1980).

Foy, Eddie, and Alvin Harlow. *Clowning Through Life*. New York: E.P. Dutton & Company, 1928.

Franzi, Emil, "Wyatt Earp's Last Deputy," *Tucson Weekly* (August 27–September 2, 1998).

Gamblers, The. Alexandria, Virginia: Time-Life Books, 1978.

Gipson, Rosemary. *The History of Tucson Theatre Before 1906: An M.A. Thesis Submitted to the Faculty of the Department of Drama*. Master of Arts, University of Arizona, 1967.

Harris, Charles, and Buck Rainey. *The Cowboy: Six-shooters, Songs, and Sex*. Norman: University of Oklahoma Press, 1975.

Hattich, William. *Pioneer Magic*. New York: Vantage Press, 1964.

———. *Tombstone*. Norman, Oklahoma: University of Oklahoma Press, 1981.

Harwood, Hinton. *The Handbook to Arizona: Its Resources, History, Towns, Mines, Ruins, and Scenery*. Glorieta, New Mexico: Rio Grande Press, 1970.

Helldorado, 1879–1929: The Semi-Centennial Celebration of the Founding of the Famous

Mining Camp of Tombstone, Arizona. Tombstone: Tombstone Epitaph, 1999.

Isenberg, Michael. *John L. Sullivan and His America.* Urbana: University of Illinois Press, 1994.

Jahns, Pat. *The Frontier World of Doc Holliday.* New York: Hastings House Publishers, 1979.

Jervey, Edward, "Methodism in Arizona: The First Seventy Years," *Arizona and the West* (Winter 1961).

Kelley, Edward J., "Tombstone Sketches," *Arizona Highways* (August 1932).

Kelly, William. *Gamblers of the Old West: Gambling Men and Women of the 1880s.* Las Vegas: B & F Enterprises, 1995.

Lake, Stuart. *Wyatt Earp: Frontier Marshal.* Boston: Houghton Mifflin Co., 1931.

Laurie, Joe. *Vaudeville: From the Honky-Tonks to the Palace.* New York: Henry Holt and Company, 1953.

Ledbetter, Suzann. *Nellie Cashman: Prospector and Trailblazer.* El Paso: Texas Western Press, 1993.

Love, Frank. *Mining Camps and Ghost Towns: A History of Mining in Arizona and California Along the Lower Colorado.* Los Angeles: Westernlore Press, 1974.

MacMinn, George R. *The Theater of the Golden Era in California.* Caldwell, Idaho: The Caxton Printers, 1941.

Mancini, John, "Fort Huachuca on the Arizona Frontier Was Home to Famous Buffalo Soldiers," *Wild West* (October 1992).

Marks, Paula Mitchell. *And Die in the West: The Story of the O.K. Corral Gunfight.* Norman: University of Oklahoma Press, 1989.

Martin, Cy. *Whiskey and Wild Women: An Amusing Account of the Saloons and Bawds of the Old West.* New York: Hart Publishing Company, 1974.

Martin, Douglas. *Silver, Sex and Six Guns: Tombstone Saga of the Life of Buckskin Frank Leslie.* Tombstone: Tombstone Epitaph, 1962.

———. *Tombstone's Epitaph.* Norman: University of Oklahoma Press, 1997.

McCool, Grace. *Gunsmoke: The True Story of Old Tombstone.* Tucson: Treasure Chest Publications, 1990.

Miners, The. Alexandria, Virginia: Time–Life Books, 1976.

Mintz, Lawrence, "Humor and Ethnic Stereotypes in Vaudeville and Burlesque," *MELUS* (Winter 1996).

Muscatine, Doris. *Old San Francisco: The Biography of a City.* New York: G.P. Putnam's Sons, 1975.

Myers, John Myers. *Tombstone's Early Years.* Lincoln: University of Nebraska Press, 1995.

Peterson, Thomas H. *The Tombstone Stagecoach Lines, 1878–1903: A Thesis Submitted to the Faculty of the Department of History.* Master of Arts, University of Arizona. Tucson, 1968.

Rickards, Colin. *Buckskin Frank Leslie: Gunman of Tombstone.* El Paso: Texas Western College Press, 1964.

Rochlin, Harriet, and Fred Rochlin. *Pioneer Jews.* Boston: Houghton Mifflin, 1984.

Rogers, W. Lane, ed. *When All Roads Led to Tombstone: A Memoir by John Pleasant Gray.* Boise: Tamarack Books, 1998.

Rosa, Joseph. *The Gunfighter: Man or Myth.* Norman: University of Oklahoma Press, 1969.

Ryan, Pat. *Tombstone Theatre Tonight: A Chronicle of Entertainment on the Southwestern Mining Frontier.* Tucson: The Tucson Corral of the Westerners, 1966. Part of the series "The Smoke Signal."

Sanders, John R., "Faro: Favorite Gambling Game of the Frontier," *Wild West* (October 1996).

Seagraves, Anne. *Soiled Doves: Prostitution in the Early West*. Hayden, Idaho: Wesanne Publications, 1994.

Shadegg, Stephen, "Cards, Gentlemen," *Arizona Highways* (February 1944).

Sharlet, Jeff, "Author's Methods Lead to Showdown Over Much-Admired Book on Old West," *The Chronicle of Higher Education* (June 11, 1999).

Sonnichsen, Charles L. *Billy King's Tombstone: The Private Life of an Arizona Boom Town*. Caldwell, Idaho: The Caxton Printers, 1942.

Spitz, Jill Jorden, "Mudslingers of the O.K. Corral," *The Arizona Daily Star*, July 24, 1998.

Stephens, John, ed. *Wyatt Earp Speaks*. Cambria Pines by the Sea, California: Fern Canyon Press, 1998.

Story of the Bird Cage. Tombstone: Epitaph Press, 1929.

Tefertiller, Casey. *Wyatt Earp: The Life Behind the Legend*. New York: John Wiley & Sons, 1997.

Toll, Robert C. *On With the Show: The First Century of Show Business in America*. New York: Oxford University Press, 1976.

Townsmen, The. Alexandria, Virginia: Time–Life Books, 1975.

Traywick, Ben T. *The Chinese Dragon in Tombstone*. Tombstone: Red Marie's Bookstore, 1989.

———. *The Chronicles of Tombstone*. Tombstone: Red Marie's Bookstore, 1994.

———. *Eleanora Dumont, Alias Madam Moustache*. Tombstone: Red Marie's Bookstore, 1990.

———. *Hell's Belles of Tombstone*. Tombstone: Red Marie's Bookstore, 1993.

———. *Historical Documents and Photographs of Tombstone*. Tombstone: Red Marie's Bookstore, 1988.

———. *Legendary Characters of Southeast Arizona*. Tombstone: Red Marie's Bookstore, 1992.

———. "Tombstone's Bird Cage," in *Best of the Wild West*. Harrisburg, Pennsylvania: Cowles Publishers, 1996.

Trimble, Marshall. *Arizona: A Cavalcade of History*. Tucson: Treasure Chest Publications, 1989.

———. *In Old Arizona: True Tales of the Wild Frontier*. Phoenix: Golden West Publishers, 1993.

Tritten, Larry, "On the Trail of Wyatt Earp," *American Legion Magazine* (October 1994).

Waters, Frank. *The Earp Brothers of Tombstone*. Lincoln: University of Nebraska Press, 1976.

Way, W. J. *The Tombstone Story*. Tombstone: W. John Way, 1965.

Willson, Claire E. *Mimes and Miners: A Historical Study of the Theater in Tombstone*. Tucson: 1935.

———. "Pioneer Playhouse of Tombstone," *Arizona Highways* (October 1939).

Wister, Fanny, ed. *Owen Wister Out West: His Journals and Letters*. Chicago: University of Chicago Press, 1958.

Wood, Ted. *Ghosts of the Southwest: The Phantom Gunslinger and Other Real-Life Hauntings*. New York: Walker and Company, 1997.

Zeidman, Irving. *The American Burlesque Show*. New York: Hawthorn Books, 1967.

Index

(*Note:* italic page numbers indicate photographs.)

Printed in the United States
134508LV00003B/31/A